THE ELMWATER
PROJECT

CLIFFORD MORRIS

Publishing Coordinator – Sharon Kizziah-Holmes

Paperback-Press
an imprint of A & S Publishing
A & S Holmes, Inc.

ISBN -13: 978-1-945669-85-9

ACKNOWLEDGMENTS

I want to thank Linda Hull, Allyn Collins, Bob Strange, John Morris, Joe Kulbiski, Don Cecil, Bill Wetterman and all the writers and editors of TulsaNightwriters for all their comments and suggestions in the development of this story.

"People are so simple and willing to obey present emotions rather than search for the truth that a person who deceives will always find those who allow themselves to be deceived." Machiavelli

CHAPTER ONE

TWO MEN DRANK KARAK CHAI spiced tea at a Benghazi outdoor café and pondered their next move. After years of waiting, bribing, manipulating, and hoping, Allah had answered their prayers. They had acquired the fissionable material. A cooperative Pakistani general obtained the weapons-grade uranium, a total of one hundred kilos, packed in two separate containers now loaded on an ocean vessel at the port of Karachi as part of a shipment of rice. The general was paid two million dollars in U.S. currency.

Asim Maroun lit a Turkish cigarette and inhaled deeply. He took a sip of his tea, leaned across the table, and spoke softly over his cup. "In forty days the ship will be in the Gulf of Mexico. The ship's regular port is Houston, but as you directed, we have men in Biloxi and Port Arthur if we have to change plans."

Gregory Mendenhall focused his gaze beyond Asim's shoulder. He studied the foot traffic as it passed in front of the café. Mendenhall, German by birth, converted to Islam in Saudi Arabia where his father worked as a petroleum engineer. Fluent in four languages, he easily passed as an American when he traveled abroad. Mendenhall was in charge of the operation precisely because he was not Arab. He could interact with foreigners in ways the Arab team members could not.

Both of the men had taken part in the assault on the American embassy that killed every person defending the consulate. In the years since the fall of Kadafi and the country's fall into turmoil, Al-Qaeda in Libya had grown. The terrorists raked in millions selling the country's crude oil on the black market.

"And the assembly team?" Mendenhall asked.

"They are all in Kansas City, ready to move," Asim said. "As soon as the shipment arrives, I will be there with them. We intend to prepare one suitcase for New York, one for Chicago, one for Los Angeles, and one for Houston." His eyes lit with excitement at his pronouncement.

"Won't they be too heavy to carry down the street?"

"I thought of that. We may need to use cars or delivery trucks," Asim said.

Mendenhall sat quietly, contemplating. So many things could go wrong. There were many details to consider. Acquiring radioactive material was a big step, but the work had only begun.

"I can see it," Asim said, "in the heart of large cities, the initial blast contained by skyscrapers. Every street will become a tunnel of death. Seconds later, every structure within a mile will implode into dust."

Mendenhall closed his eyes and rubbed his temples as though applying massage might bring forth a critical detail he had thus far overlooked. He plowed his brain for any last kernel of inspiration. He opened his eyes and exhaled audibly. "How many people do you think these devices will kill?"

"I don't know exactly," Asim said. " If there are say, around 100,000 people in these U.S. cities downtown areas every workday, then the number of infidels sent to hell would be massive."

"We have to come up with something better," Mendenhall finally said, shaking his head. "Suitcases and delivery trucks won't do. Yes – we would kill thousands that way, but we wouldn't kill the right ones."

ON THE HIGH PLAINS of the Kansas prairie, a curious sight greeted the townspeople of Elmwater, Kansas. People pointed, chuckled, gossiped, and scratched their heads. At daybreak, news of the spectacle spread faster than the prairie wind before a summer rain. Main Street became a parking lot, blocked curb to curb. The sight was both funny and disturbing. Anyone with a sharp eye could see the potential danger that lurked in the tilting monstrosity that blocked the street.

During the overnight hours, Andy Branson and his crew worked to move an ancient two-story Victorian home to a new foundation five miles outside of town. It was additional work for Andy to supplement his farming income. The thirty-foot railroad ties placed under the house had rested laterally across a forty-foot trailer. A sharp turn taken onto MainStreet caused the weight of the tall structure to shift. An outside tire blew, and in slow motion, the house began to slide. The shifting weight rocked the trailer sideways. The house slid off the beams until the lower edge of an outside wall touched the street. A rusty weathervane atop the gabled roof leaned, stopping mere inches from an overhead wire.

The house sat in the town's main intersection. The tire couldn't be changed until they leveled the load. Andy called around for any available wenches, jacks, and tractors. The Co-Op had two front-end loaders they could spare. Jake at the junkyard volunteered the use of his wrecker. With a combined effort, the men might be able to lift the cantilevered railroad ties, thus the weight of the house, and maneuver it back onto the trailer.

Andy had plenty on his mind without the added pressure when the leaning house became a sideshow. The barber dragged a straight-backed chair outside and cut hair on the sidewalk. Aides rolled the residents of the nursing home to the edge of the parking lot where they could see the scene from half a block away. The elementary school principal, Mr. Collins, decided to allow a school outing so everyone could get a closer look at the curious sight. Along with the other teachers, Missy Eckles led her second-grade class downtown. The children pointed, and jumped, and talked as they walked toward town.

The crowd continued to grow. Mae Morgan quickly ran out of donuts and brewed coffee at the grocery store. Robby Dawes, the photographer for the town's weekly newspaper, *The Schooner,* snapped more pictures than he'd ever need. But snap away he did, from every conceivable angle including underneath the upraised side of the house. Then he climbed to the roof of Neal's Pharmacy and snapped a dozen more. Old man Kirby shook his fist and swore in the driveway of his Phillips 66. Parked vehicles blocked both entrances into his station. No one could get in to buy gas.

For a country town of 1,856 people, the house in the street was a sight that no one would soon forget. School teachers talked among themselves. The adults were as awestruck as the children. Many of the boys drifted away from the class groups to get a better look and study the sight up close. Several of them got on their knees and crawled under the house. Seeing the underside of a house was a discovery unto itself, and the boys marveled at the thick beams and the maze of crisscrossed timbers.

Seconds later, the house dropped. The side wall buckled an inch or two.

"Look!" someone cried.

Missy turned as an ominous gasp rolled through the crowd.

"Oh, my god," came an anguished voice.

"Get them out," screamed another.

The house had settled a fraction. A low octave groan of stressed, twisted lumber reverberated up from the bowels of the structure as though the house itself were crying for help. One boy covered in dust scrambled from under the house. The weathervane dropped further and cut a telephone wire in two. Everyone held their breath as though the slightest vibration might cause the ancient structure of wood and plaster to implode upon itself. It didn't. But it had fallen enough, and second-grader, Taylor Carson was trapped underneath.

CHAPTER TWO

AT THE SAME TIME, a green sedan with tinted windows exited the state highway and drove toward the center of town. The lone occupant saw the house in the street and the crowd around it. He turned down a side street. His interest was a single destination that shouldn't be hard to find, The Farmers State Bank.

The bank's sign could be seen from two blocks away. Gregory Mendenhall parked at the far end of the lot. The interior of the bank conveyed a bygone scene with wooden teller windows trimmed in tarnished brass. Dim glass globes hung from twenty-foot ceilings. The transaction counters, the doors, even the floor was all walnut and oak. The place smelled of Pine Sol. A matronly woman at the first teller window took his name and promptly escorted him to a back office.

Ralph Whitmire, the bank president, extended his hand as he stepped from behind his massive desk. "Mr. Mendenhall, it's a pleasure to meet you. Won't you sit down?"

Without a word, Mendenhall shook Whitmire's hand, took a seat, and placed his attache case beside it. He folded his hands under his chin and rubbed his index fingers against his lower lip. "As I mentioned on the phone, your town of Elmwater has been chosen to receive a federal grant for civic capital improvements. The United States government knows small towns have infrastructure needs just like larger communities, along with repairs, maintenance, and updating."

"As the only bank in town, we would like you to supervise the disbursement of funds for properly authorized projects and keep adequate records."

Whitmire sat transfixed, basking in Mendenhall's enticing story. This government man was talking about his favorite subject. Whitmire was a third-generation president of the bank. If making money was at the heart of this discussion, he was ready to play ball. His avarice was exceeded only by the girth of his belly. He was impressed by this visitor from Washington. Whitmire also knew how to play the game. He wanted to hear some numbers because he wasn't going to flip cartwheels and promote their agenda for a few token deposits into his bank. Whitmire waited patiently to listen to the rest of the story.

"We would also like the bank to extend credit to current residents," Mendenhall continued, "so they can start or expand small businesses, purchase new equipment, repair or remodel homes. The program is designed to run for three years. We'd like to see Elmwater thriving by that time."

"Sounds like an excellent idea," Whitmire said.

"I'll be talking to the city fathers, and then there'll be an announcement made to everyone in town. If a majority of citizens approve the measure, Elmwater will be officially in the program – Renew-Repair-Revitalize."

Whitmire sat forward and nodded approvingly as his jowls bounced on his jaw.

"There's one bit of information I need to get from you today, Mr. Whitmire. What is the current value of your outstanding loans?"

"Well, ah," Whitmire hesitated. "Unless you're a regulator, that's confidential information."

Mendenhall's eyes narrowed. His face tightened, but his voice remained calm and assuring. "A ballpark figure is all I need. Round numbers will be fine."

"Well, let's see." Whitmire pulled a leather-bound ledger from his desk drawer. "We have around sixty family farms that are our largest borrowers. They borrow to buy feeder pigs and calves and pay back the loans when they've gone to market. It's the same with seed and fertilizer for planting with repayment at harvest. Lots of corn and wheat grown in these parts. Along with business and personal loans, the bank's portfolio is right at I'd say, forty million."

"Fine," Mendenhall said as he opened the brass latches on his attache case. "I have here an official commitment to your bank to be the fiduciary for this program." He pulled a document from his case stamped with a red, white, and blue seal and signed although the signature was unreadable. "Disbursal of funds will begin after I've contacted all city officials, and agreements such as this one are approved."

Mendenhall waited for it to be signed, then he leaned across Whitmire's desk and looked directly into his eyes. "Now, if you change your mind and wish not to be a part of this program, that's fine. But let me be clear, this conversation is not to leave this room regardless of your decision. Are there any questions about that?"

"No, I understand. That's perfectly agreeable."

Mendenhall took the signed document from Whitmire and handed him another piece of paper. "That will be the amount available to your community?" Mendenhall's detached business demeanor remained unchanged.

Whitmire perused the document. His eyes widened. His mouth fell open. "Oh, yes, oh, yes. This is quite generous."

"I'll be back in touch with you soon," Mendenhall said then stood and left the room.

Whitmire didn't even notice Mendenhall had gone. All he could do was blink and stare in awe at the paper in front of him. "Fifty million dollars," he muttered, "fifty million."

CHAPTER THREE

⬤

THE DOWNTOWN ATMOSPHERE around the tilting house changed abruptly from festive to somber as though someone had flipped a switch. Adults grabbed any child near them, and a wide circle of space appeared around the crumbling structure as though the Red Sea had parted in the middle of the street. The house buckled under a severe lean. The old timbers couldn't stand the stress. Unseen boards cracked and split with anguished snaps. The house had fallen enough to trap the little boy and prevent his escape.

Andy sprinted to the trailer and dropped to his knees on the high side of the listing house. Andy could see the boy's green shirt though his face was turned away. Broken floorboards jutted down and prevented the boy's movement. Taylor didn't appear hurt, only trapped. The boy was nearer to the other side of the trailer, but the flat tire blocked access to him. Andy jumped to his feet. "Dan!"

"Right here, boss."

"We've got to get that far side up."

"There's no clearance for the jacks," Dan replied. "None of the front end loaders are here yet. Jake's wrecker is though. There might be enough room to get his cable in there to clear the boy."

"Okay. Hook it up under the beam beside the flat tire. I'm going back in." Andy grabbed a battery powered circular saw from his truck and ducked under the trailer.

Missy stood nearby and listened to the men. She called out to the boy. "Taylor, it won't take long to get you out. Be strong. You'll be out soon."

Another horrible ripping noise rumbled through the house. Window shutters on the lower side dangled open. The rusty weathervane atop the highest gable finally broke loose and crashed into the street. Built of solid 4 X 4" oak posts, the ancient structure might well have stood another hundred years if left alone, but the move from its original foundation proved more than the stack of dried boards could endure.

Andy cut jagged wood out of his way and crawled in ever-tightening space toward the boy. Dust sifted over him. Before long, he was doing everything by feel. He reached the boy, touched his back, and received a whimper in return. The boy was on his stomach, trapped by a board across his legs. Andy tried to lift it, to push it away, but it wouldn't budge.

From the street, onlookers saw the wall bow outward as the house slid sideways, further off the trailer. Jake had the wrecker in place. Dan pulled the slack cable and dropped it down to Andy. He yanked the hawser under the beam and thrust it up where Dan could reach it and lock the hook.

"Straight up, Dan," Andy yelled. "Straight up."

The winch turned, the slack cable wound on the drum. The motor groaned. Jake gave the engine more gas., The creosote railroad tie rose, lifting the floorboards. The side of the house shifted forward as it ascended.

As the side of the house rose, the winch struggled. It hummed a deep baritone. Space appeared above the flat tire. The board across the boy's legs rose several inches. Andy pushed with his feet as hard as he could as though his toenails might claw through his boots to get closer to the boy, grab his belt, and pull him free. The house was barely moving higher now. The winch began ticking. Andy's focus was on the boy. Ripping sounds throughout the house sent an involuntary chill up his spine. He and the boy were in an echo chamber of snapping boards and splitting beams.

He got a tight grip on the boy's belt and began the arduous effort to move backward, away from the low side of the house. Andy pulled as hard as he could. He scratched his way out, away from the smoke of the whining winch. The taut cable hummed like a swarm of angry bees.

"Get out!" Dan screamed.

The wrecker cable managed to lift the side of the

two-story house almost a foot. When the cable broke, it sounded like a bomb went off. Railroad ties smashed onto the steel trailer. The house quaked with a visible tremor. Half of the house collapsed upon itself, and a section of the second-story roof sailed onto Hershner's Auto Parts plate glass window.

Andy pulled his chin to his chest and covered his face with one arm. A chunk of plaster cracked him in the back of the head. Taylor cut loose with an agonizing scream as a splintered 2 X 4 stabbed him in the back. They were both covered with broken lathe and plaster. Andy still had a grip on the boy, but he could no longer move.

At street level, the living room wall crumbled, open entirely to view. Through the doorway to the kitchen, tall white cabinets could be seen lying in a stack like broken boxes. A double-wide porcelain sink dangled on the back wall. The attic ripped open. Dust and insulation spilled forth in a choking cloud. The remaining half of the house teetered on the trailer, off balance, without a counterweight, rocked and swayed. Exposed ends of the railroad ties, now without any meaningful weight on them, rose through the broken structure like the ends of a giant teeter-tauter. In a final statement of surrender, what remained of the house fell off the other side of the trailer, and crumbled into Kirby's 66 service station.

Andy held his breath, listening to the death throes of the house. He struggled to get to his elbows. Although unhurt, both he and the boy were trapped. There was a moment of relief when the noise abated, then worry as he no longer heard sounds from the youngster.

"Talk to us, Andy," Dan yelled.

"We're on this side," Andy hollered back as loud as he could with his face down, inches above the street. "I'm right here with the boy. Get this crap off us."

The crowd jumped to the urgent task to free them before they smothered. Andy spat grit and dust from his tongue. A shaft of light appeared at the corner of his eye. A dozen hands pulled at the broken boards that held them down. Dan helped Andy to a sitting position, and for several minutes, he sat in the rubble, catching his breath.

Beneath a coat of dust and grime, young Taylor was limp and quiet. There was a gash on his head; the back of his shirt was bloody. Taylor was unconscious as townfolk carried him to the ambulance. Everyone in the town square watched dumbstruck as the ambulance sped away engulfed in flashing lights with siren blaring.

Andy drank from an offered bottle of water and tried to shake the dirt from his hair.

"You'd better let them check you over at the hospital," Dan suggested.

"Whatever . . . just take me to the truck."

Andy wobbled as he crossed the street. A ringing persisted in his ears. His jeans were torn down the right leg. Dust caked his entire body. A cut on his forehead bled down the bridge of his nose, and the welt on the back of his head became noticeable.

"Come on, Andy, let's get you to the doc," Dan said.

As the men got in the truck, Missy approached Andy's open door.

"I'm the boy's teacher," she said. Andy looked at her through glassy eyes. "We're so thankful for what you did."

Andy dabbed the bloody bridge of his nose and stared at her in disgust. "I didn't do anything, lady. We were lucky to get the boy out. If you're his teacher, you should have been watching him. If you had done your job, we might not have lost the house. Come on, Dan, let's go." He slammed the door.

THE ELEMENTARY SCHOOL PRINCIPAL, Mr. Collins, directed the teachers to get the students back to the schoolhouse. Collins raced to the hospital right behind the fading wails of emergency sirens. He'd make sure Taylor's parents were notified of the disastrous event once he was there, but deep inside he was reasonably sure they already knew. Elmwater was a close-knit town. Any news worth knowing spread instantly. Anyone who didn't hear it was either deaf or asleep.

The hospital had been built on a hill in the 1930s, of earth-red brick with yellow limestone corners and mantels. Visitors to the main entrance had to ascend a series of broad steps. But the rise was gradual, the climb easy, and the approach through interlocking branches and overgrown ivy was a walk through a tunnel of shade. A separate, curved drive wound around to the back of the building to the emergency entrance. The hospital had twenty-four rooms, each defended by a massive seven-foot oak door with a brass handle. For ninety years, Elmwater Memorial had served the needs of the community. The town hadn't grown, so the facility continued to meet its needs.

Dan drove Andy to the emergency entrance, but all attention in the ER focused on Taylor Carson. The men had to park at the back of the lot and wait fifteen minutes before a nurse approached them. Andy held a handkerchief to his bloody forehead. He moaned off and on, seated in a stiff waiting-room chair, his eyes closed.

"Okay, who's hurt and how bad?" asked the elderly nurse. Her name was Ruth, and she was a hospital relic – efficient, empathetic, and no-nonsense all rolled up in one person.

"It's Andy. He got hurt in the same accident as the boy. He needs stitches, and I think he has a concussion," Dan said.

"Let's go in this room." She said. "Take your shirt off. I'll have the doctor in soon."

Soon turned into thirty minutes. When the doctor showed, his frazzled appearance and pale complexion were impossible to miss. Andy and Dan glanced at each other. The doctor's mind was preoccupied, but he tended to Andy's wounds. Using local anesthetic, he gave Andy three stitches above his right eye, told him to put some ice on the welt on the back of his head, and get some rest. He took no more time with Andy than it would take to brand a calf and pronounced him strong as an ox. The doctor pulled off his sterile gloves, threw them in the wastebasket, and left the room without another word.

Andy put his shirt on and was ready to take the doctor's advice and get some rest. Dan could handle the mess downtown and get the trailer back to his farm. Most likely the city was already hauling away the broken down house and sweeping the street, ready to send Andy a hefty bill for the cleanup. But all thoughts of the house vanished from Andy's mind when he and Dan stepped into the emergency room waiting area.

Inconsolable sobs bubbled up from the group of people gathered there. And as they made their way to the back door, Andy overheard a man on a cell phone.

"The medical staff worked on Taylor for more than an hour, but he didn't make it. Taylor was pronounced dead shortly after ten."

BY THREE IN THE AFTERNOON Mendenhall had located Delbert Lupton (everyone called him Del) the town mayor. Del was a short man with bushy white eyebrows, a city councilman for fifteen years, and a nervous wreck when it came to considering new ideas. He was made aware that funds for capital improvements were being made available for his town. It struck him as no great leap of logic to accept the notion that the federal government had extra money to burn. Free money for the town was a proposition he could swallow. But when the proviso of absolute confidentiality was stressed to him not once, but three times, Del became anxious.

By the end of the day, two prominent men in the community had been informed and overwhelmed with the news. Banker Ralph Whitmire was as ecstatic as a hummingbird hovering over a honeysuckle blossom on a calm day. Mayor Del Lupton, on the other hand, was thrown into a dither. He was terrified he'd violated some city ordinance by okaying the commitment without first holding a city council meeting.

So, Del set out to do just that. He called the other two city councilmen, Buster Warren, and Colton Garrison. He didn't reveal details, but his tone was grave. He told the other two men in no uncertain terms that they had to meet in an emergency session. The disaster created by the demise of the Victorian house was secondary to what they now had to consider. They agreed to meet at seven sharp, but stayed near their phones, calling each other back and forth into the wee hours of the morning.

MENDENHALL DROVE A HUNDRED MILES back to a rented townhouse in Salina. He threw his suit jacket on the bed and took off his shoes, then loosened his tie and sat back with a cup of hibiscus tea. He enjoyed playing the part of a government agent. Keeping a rein on a herd of sunburnt plowboys shouldn't be that hard to do. He needed to stay close to the action and make sure the townspeople were all preoccupied. At the same time, he would be close to the real project and be able to keep tabs on its progress.

He was in charge of the operation. Experts were part of the team to handle the precision work. The day had gone well. He laughed at the thought of how people scramble like rats when a few dollar bills get tossed into the breeze from an upper story window. With the money he had available, he would have the people of Elmwater, Kansas, as pliant as warm taffy when the funds began flowing.

Mendenhall's parents were German, but he never knew his homeland. The faith of his parent's upbringing was Anglican, but they were agnostic in a foreign land. His father moved his family to Saudi Arabia for the work, and the money. As a petroleum engineer, he was well paid. He cared nothing for the Saudi's dress, their grating language, or their god-forsaken desert. His mother remained in the home.

But Gregory Mendenhall was raised in the madrassas of Saudi Arabia. Every day in school, he recited the Koran. Over time, the memorization of the text became a balm to his soul. The holy scriptures gave him answers to his purpose in life, the order of things, his place in it all. He made friends, learned the culture, and enjoyed the food. By the time he was in his teens, Mendenhall was a zealot for Allah. His faith ran deep nurtured in tradition and ceremony. The jihadist took notice. He was a prized and welcomed addition into their fold.

At 7:00 p.m., he called Kansas City. After one ring, the phone someone answered. No salutation. No small talk. "How'd it go?"

"Just as planned. No problems I could detect. Mention free money, and they snap to attention."

"What projects did they have in mind?"

"I told the mayor to come up with a prioritized list. Didn't get into details, but I can have construction up and running within two weeks."

"Did you bring up the water tower?"

"I'll take care of that," Mendenhall said, a bit peeved at the unnecessary questions. "I have everything under control here. I'm more concerned about your end."

"We're ready. Just waiting for the shipment to arrive. Wichita is already at work."

"Okay, give me another week, and you can have trucks rolling. I'll call back in three days, same time."

Mendenhall hung up. Physically and emotionally, his body had been wired tight for weeks, would be for weeks to come. His mind was stressed though he didn't realize it. He wouldn't have acknowledged his need for rest even if the thought had crossed his mind. But as he lay back on the bed, he was asleep in seconds, still fully clothed.

CHAPTER FOUR

THE NEXT DAY, Andy awoke sore, stiff, and generally miserable. He hadn't slept, and it wasn't from the pain of the gash on his head. He couldn't stop thinking about the boy. The anguish ran deep as though he'd lost a child of his own. One of the times when the house settled, a splintered board stabbed little Taylor, which ultimately led to his death. Andy thought he'd pulled him free of danger. He blamed himself for all that happened though he knew the fact that the boy ventured under the house wasn't his fault. That knowledge did nothing to ease his sense of guilt.

Andy walked out to his shed, a 20' X 30' Quonset hut built next to his dilapidated barn. Shortly after nine, the phone in the shed began to ring. Evelyn Keaton called from city hall to tell him to expect a bill for the cleanup of the street. The Hershners called to learn how he planned to pay for a new plate glass window. Old man Kirby threatened a lawsuit for lost income at his gas station.

Andy sat down the phone and closed his eyes. He'd lost a substantial chunk of his income and more importantly, his reputation. Cal Johnson called last night and canceled his job. Andy knew full well Cal was going to move a half dozen old barracks from the abandoned air base and turn them into horse stalls. Cal hadn't canceled the move. The call meant Cal was going to get someone else to do it. Andy still had the job of hauling scrap metal from the Cooper Machine Works to Salina. But that two hundred miles round trip was required only twice a month. Andy didn't expect anyone to call anytime soon for new moving or hauling jobs.

Andy looked over the old farmhouse, the only place he'd known as home. He had an older sister who doted on him when they were younger, but with whom he had little in common when they reached their teenage years. She liked books. She had no interest in remaining in a farm town. A move to the big city was in her long-term plans. She was married now, living in Ohio.

Andy was happy where he was. Farm work wasn't easy, but he liked the wide open spaces, a blanket of snow that stretched as far as the eye could see in winter, the vast acres of green fields of growing crops in the spring.

His dad taught him something about everything. If he had a question, his dad would take all the time it took to provide an answer. If his dad didn't know, he'd help Andy find an answer. His dad taught him how to hunt, to birth a calf, and drive a tractor. From his dad, he saw how to treat a woman. Never hurts to pay them a compliment, he often said. Be appreciative and show it. His dad was much more than just appreciative of his mother.

With daily farm chores and summers of bucking bales, Andy grew robust and fast. He received a football scholarship to attend Kansas State University where he majored in Agri-business. His junior year he made the varsity playing outside linebacker for the Wildcats. One week he intercepted a screen pass against Texas Tech and ran it back for a touchdown. The following week, he got blindsided by a crackback block and tore his ACL. His season was over.

A month later, his mother died unexpectedly. He attended the funeral with his entire leg in a cast. Rehabilitation on the knee went poorly. For ten months he worked to maintain his class schedule and regain mobility in his knee. But he never recovered the strength or speed he once possessed. The end of his football career had arrived.

After graduation, Andy returned to Elmwater to help his dad on the farm once again. For five more years they worked together until his father passed away. The place was now his, and that was fine with Andy. He would keep the farm and work the land. His dad had been a lifelong farmer, and if the lifestyle was good enough for his dad, it was good enough for him.

Andy saw Dan's beat-up Dodge Ram with its

bed jammed full of junk drive up to the shed. Dan got out of the truck with a cola in one hand, a candy bar in the other.

"Nothing to do today, Dan. I'm glad we got the truck and trailer back here but, the city's going to charge me for the mess they had to clean up. Plus dump fees, and whatever else they can think of. I'm taking the day off."

The two men looked quietly at each other for a few moments.

"How's your head?" Dan asked.

"Hurts, but I'll live. Thanks for getting me to the doc."

"Sure, Andy." Dan paced in place. "I know everything's come down hard on you, Andy, but I gotta talk to you." Dan inhaled the rest of his candy bar and washed it down with a gulp of pop.

When Dan spoke again, his words came out in a rush. "I've always liked working for you, Andy. You're a real swell guy to work for, Andy, like I said, but I can go to work for Billy Conrady for more money. I went by and asked him, and he said yes. I had to, Andy. I don't know if you're gonna be able to keep busy."

Andy looked up, calm, and reflective. His bright blue eyes shown in the morning light. He had a way of dealing with danger or bad news with a clear head, without blaming others, knowing that many things that happen turn out happening for the best. Still, he felt like he was at the bottom of a pile of football players scrambling for a fumble. "I understand, Dan," he said. "If I were in your shoes, I'd probably do the same thing."

For a moment, Dan stood in place. He'd delivered his speech. Andy could see he was stuck, wanting to go, but sorry he had to.

"I'll be seeing you around, Dan. You're a good employee."

"Thanks, Andy." With that, he turned and left.

Andy's thoughts returned to the Carson family. He had to go and express his condolences. He knew it wouldn't ease his guilt. His appearance might be unwelcome, but he had to go. He could still see little Taylor under the house. He couldn't have weighed more than a sack of potatoes. Andy couldn't shake the sadness. Seven years old. The number stuck in his mind. What a beautiful age to be alive, aware of the world but only beginning to learn, explore, discover, and spread one's wings. Everything about yesterday was a disaster. When the day ended, the loss of the house meant nothing, but the death of little Taylor was something he'd never forget.

He knew making an appearance at the funeral home was probably not the best decision he'd ever made. The family needed time alone. Anyone who saw him there would shun him if for no other reason than to not make a spectacle of his presence and further upset the mourning family. But he had to go.

His impulsive nature always got him in trouble. That was why the house move proved so disastrous. He tried to get the job done before everything was in place. For such an old and unwieldy house, more exterior supports had been needed. He should have placed vertical braces around the base to keep it from leaning. Straps that ran the length and width of the house through open windows would have provided strength against weight shifting. A better route would have avoided the sharp turn in the middle of town. But once the house had been jacked up and set on the beams, Andy was ready to go. His haste cost him lost revenue, a damaged reputation, and a dead child.

CHAPTER FIVE

THAT SAME MORNING, Missy's phone rang at her apartment before seven. She was on the couch, fully awake, having spent the night in fits of choking sobs filled with anguished tears. She answered and heard Mr. Collins' voice on the line. "We're letting the children take the day off, Miss Eckles. The board thinks it's best. We'll resume classes Monday, but all the teachers are to report as usual. I need you to come to my office when you get in." With that, he hung up.

Missy shuffled to the bathroom in a state of utter exhaustion. A glance in the mirror revealed bloodshot eyes and a runny nose. The sadness brought on by the knowledge of Taylor's death was bad enough, but the sense of guilt was enough to knock her into another sobbing heap. With great effort, she took a shower, dressed, applied her makeup, and left her apartment for the short walk to the school.

As she stood in Mr. Collins' office, she knew deep inside the outcome of the meeting. Why couldn't he send her a letter and let her disappear? Surely he would spare no words in emphasizing her culpability in Taylor's death while minimizing his own. When she came into the building only her friend, another second-grade teacher, Rita Henshaw, acknowledged her presence. Rita hugged her and told her everything would be all right. The words were empty and meaningless, and Rita seemed to know it as soon as they left her lips. Everyone else she passed glanced away. Her colleagues now treated her like a leper. She was the newest teacher in the school, and she was the boy's homeroom teacher. If anyone in town wanted to blame someone for the boy's death, they could blame her.

Mr. Collins entered from a side door and asked Missy to be seated. "I know we're barely a month into the new school year, but I want to be completely upfront with you," Collins said. He cleared his throat. "The board met in special session last night. They want to let you go." Collins placed his elbows on the desk and interlocked his fingers.

"I told them I had no replacements. I told them we had to keep you for now. I know it's going to be tough for a while, but I'm on your side, and maybe the board will change their minds. It was all a tragic accident. I don't blame you for any of it."

"I feel so bad," Missy said. "Not thirty minutes before everyone walked downtown, Taylor told me how much he enjoyed me being his teacher." Tears spilled down her cheeks. Her body rocked with sobs. Mr. Collins handed her an entire box of tissues, knelt beside her, and patted her hand. If Collins intended to say anything more, he didn't. He didn't tell her everything would be all right or say other empty platitudes of commiseration. "You can stay in here as long as you need to," he said and left the room.

DEL DRESSED BEFORE SIX. He'd drank a whole pot of coffee by himself although he didn't need a single drop to stay awake. He negotiated his F–150 around twists and turns of a dirt road, his eyes squinting through a bug-splattered windshield. Why had he ever wanted to run for elective office? The generous offer of money for the town would seem to be good news, but Del was worried. He hadn't gotten a good hour of sleep last night.

The three men of Elmwater's city council initially decided to conduct their special meeting at the city hall beside the volunteer fire station. That would mean Evelyn Keaton would be present to record the minutes. But the three of them showing up on a weekday morning would have the ladies in the water department spreading unsubstantiated gossip as quickly as their fingers could dial the phones. They decided to meet at Nate Davis' farm where they could air the matter thoroughly, and in private.

The Davis place was a rustic ranch-style home. His wife served coffee in the den as they sat at a thick wooden table covered with a red gingham cloth. A mule deer mount occupied one wall and two pheasants, wings spread in frozen flight, on the other. Davis drank a cup of coffee with the arrivals, then excused himself to attend to additional chores.

When Davis left, Del put his half cup of coffee aside, scooted his chair closer, and leaned across the table. "I wanted to tell you everything last night, but that federal guy, quite frankly, scared the hell out of me. The way he came across." Del shook his head, relieved the initial encounter was over. "I thought he might have my phone tapped or something."

"So how much are they going to give us?" Warren asked.

"I'll get to that. Let me tell you the whole thing." Del stood and walked near the fireplace, gaze cast at the ceiling, his memory recycling the previous day's events. A chuckle of relief escaped his throat as he turned and faced his colleagues.

"From the moment I laid eyes on him, I had the willies. He didn't call or nothing. Just showed up on my doorstep. He flashed some credentials, and I thought I was in trouble with the IRS or something. I confirmed I was the mayor, and he starts talking about street, water, and sewer improvements. I thought the town was in trouble for something we did or didn't do."

"He told you right off he was a federal man?" Garrison asked.

"Yeah, showed me a badge and all. He made a big deal of it. It looked official enough to me. Got me on the defensive, you know what I mean? Some bureaucrats in Washington got nothing better to do than single out a town, they can pretty much do whatever they want. Anyway, that's what went through my mind."

"So what's the bottom line?" Warren said, "How much are they offering and what's it for?"

Del returned to the table and leaned in like he needed to whisper the next words he uttered. "Up to fifty million dollars. We've got Carte Blanche. We can choose the town projects we want to be funded" His bushy eyebrows danced. A smile cracked his lips, and he began a continuous nodding to dispel the incredulous, blank gazes that starred back at him. "That's right; any project as long as it benefits the community and puts everyone to work."

Now it was Warren's turn to get up from the table and pace the room. Del remained silent. He knew Warren was thinking things through, considering the big picture. Even though Del was the current mayor, it was Warren who was the driving force on the city council. It was Warren's positions that most influenced the decisions of the group. He ran the largest new and used car and truck dealership in the area. He dealt in quality vehicles, backed his warranties, and provided reasonably priced service. He'd learned long ago you couldn't screw people in a small town and remain in business. But he never gave in on price. He had a way of squeezing every nickel from a deal, and convince his customers he'd saved them a two hundred mile round trip to the big city where they would have paid even more.

His wife inherited half interest in the local bank, her maiden name being Whitmire. Otherwise, Warren may have left Elmwater long ago to more profitable auto dealerships and challenging political venues. But Elmwater was his wife's hometown, and the family decided to stay.

"This federal guy told me that several towns had been selected to participate in the program to improve infrastructure and community services," Del said. "He didn't tell me how or why Elmwater was selected, only that we were on the list."

"What's lacking about our infrastructure except for paving a few streets?" Garrison asked.

"Nothing," Del replied. "You know that, and I know that, but our tax base isn't growing. If the feds want to give us money, I think, we should take it."

"Hell yes, we should take it," Warren said. "The government throws money at thousands of projects around the country. Why shouldn't Elmwater get its share?"

"Okay then," Del said. "We're all in favor."

"Now what?" Warren said. "What do we need to do to get this show on the road?"

"We need to come up with a prioritized list of projects to undertake. The federal guy said there would be an official announcement and we can get started after that. Oh yeah, and we need to hold a town meeting so everyone can vote on whether or not they want to be in the program."

Warren let out with a laugh. Garrison leaned back in his chair, a smile on his face.

"Okay, let's have a town hall meeting," Warren said through incredulous chuckles. "Don't know who in their right mind would vote against free money, but we'll do it their way."

"The feds want everyone notified and involved,

that's all. Sounded like a formality the way he brought it up," Del said almost apologetically as though he'd been the brunt of a joke. He shrugged his shoulders. "It's a project, not a gift. Full employment is a goal with every able adult working either at their business or on jobs related to the new projects."

"Okay then," Warren said. "Let's have a town meeting. How about next Tuesday evening? The newspaper won't be out by then so have some flyers printed up. Make some phone calls around town. Let's make it for 7:00 p.m. Fast track this idea and get that money flowing into town."

CHAPTER SIX

A T AN OUTDOOR PATIO attached to a run-down bar in Leavenworth, Kansas, five men smoked and fiddled with their drinks. The place was a dive for barflies and devoted drunks. Every fifteen minutes or so, a middle-aged woman in thick eyelashes and heavy rouge, wearing short-shorts to accent her varicose veins came to their paint-peeled picnic table to check on them. They gave her a dollar or two each time even if they didn't order anything.

Mendenhall had assembled the men. He had the blessing of Al-Qaeda in Lybia and more than enough money to see the plan through. In the minds of jihadists, money was just another tool to meet their objectives. Cash helped cover tracks. Trails also grew faint and untraceable when washed in blood.

Gregory Mendenhall's ideology was intractable and straightforward. He was a globalist in both politics and religion. Petty spats over small pieces of territory held no interest for him. The world must be united, come together under one faith, one doctrine for living, one economic system. The hearts and minds of all men must be aligned. The old order must be destroyed, utterly annihilated. After that, the uniting could begin. Only then would Allah bless the people of the earth.

"I have laid the groundwork in the town near our site of operation. We will have food and lodging nearby, and few, if any, watchful eyes to interfere with our work," Mendenhall said. He grasped Asim Maroun's arm with two hands in a sign of strength and unity. Mendenhall knew Asim was competent, efficient, and dedicated. There was nothing Mendenhall would not entrust Asim to get done.

Mendenhall had known Asim for more than five years, and in all that time they had never spoken about any topic other than the one that brought them together again today. Asim was a physicist by training having graduated from MIT in the late '90s. He was a religious fanatic from the circumstances of his childhood. His life's work was the cause of Islam. Asim was a confident yet cautious man. No challenge was too great for him to accept. Conventional bombs were his area of expertise. Now he was soon to obtain fissionable material. He had waited twenty years for the opportunity, and when the shipment arrived, he knew how to assemble a nuclear device.

All of the men at the table had been hand-picked for their expertise in assembling and launching a rocket. Every man at the table had been at work for weeks on their area of responsibility. The purpose of the meeting was to update their progress and address any potential problems.

Mendenhall turned to two men named Hanania and Raghib. They lived in Wichita and were former Boeing employees. They were to build the rocket sections and mix the solid rocket fuel. "What's your progress?" Mendenhall asked.

"No problems. We've secured five-foot diameter PVC pipe, fiberglass mesh, and sheet metal for the skin. It will all melt and fall away when the fuel is completely burned. We're working on fuel mixtures combinations, particularly what ingredient combinations give the hottest burn."

The last man at the table was Daniel Romme. Now thirty years old, he was born in Jordon to American parents. He grew up in both Amman, Jordan and Patterson, New Jersey. He spoke Arabic and English fluently. He turned eighteen while in America and decided he wanted to join the Army. He served two tours in Afghanistan fighting the Taliban. He became 100% soldier, 100% killer. He learned how to operate tanks and heavy equipment.

But after his discharge, his patriotism waned. He became disillusioned with America's 'pursuit of happiness' slogan when he saw so many veterans abandoned in their time of need by the country they so faithfully served. He remembered the days of his youth. He knew the ways of the Middle East. Their lives were more straightforward than the hectic hustle of America. Their communities were united. The Muslim faith was stronger and demonstrated daily. Their faith was personal and the center of their lives, unlike the Americans who went through religious rituals one day a week and on occasional holidays. He fell in with a group of zealots, and within a year he was one of them.

Romme's allegiance switched to the downtrodden and dispossessed of the Muslim world. He rejected the imperialist capitalism of his parents. Mentally, he dismissed his years of service in the U.S. military. But in fact, Romme didn't discriminate. He enjoyed soldiering and fighting, so if there was a conflict and someone gave him a rifle and regular pay, he would point his weapon at whoever they called the enemy.

"Keep making your preparations," Mendenhall said. "I will return to the farm town of Elmwater here in Kansas, where we are going to make our stand."

A RUMOR DESCENDED UPON ELMWATER. No one knew the origin, what the buzz meant, or if any of it were remotely true. Free money was headed for Elmwater. Gossip like that was a conversation starter if there ever was one. Once a person got a whiff of it, everyone had an instant opinion of the best course of action.

Rick's Diner was Elmwater's early morning hangout. Coffee mugs were never empty, and the talk was cheap but never in short supply. Lifelong farmers congregated in the corner of the restaurant and gossipped worse than a dozen women over a backyard fence. Each man had an assigned and reserved seat. They talked in hushed tones while lighting cigars and pipes and jotting on pull-naps. Their conversations were occasionally pierced by explosions of laughter from someone's newly discovered joke.

The hot topic today was the rumor. Even with the collapsed house fiasco and the death of the schoolboy, the rumor was front and center on everyone's lips. By now it was more than a puff of mist drifting on the breeze. Everyone thought there was something to it. When Del Lupton hadn't shown up by seven, it was a sure sign something new was afloat.

Galen Cecil pulled on the straps of his overalls and commented on the mayor. "If I were guessing, I'd say Del's gonna keep a lid on this 'till he figures out how it'll benefit him the most, then maybe he'll let the rest of us in on it."

"And you are," Bob Michaels interjected.

"What?"

"Just guessing. Del's never conspired against anybody."

"What I mean," Galen said, his pink face growing redder, " if the town's getting an influx of money we need to be in on the decision making."

"That 'old back road' needs to be graded and blacktopped," Franklin Bates chimed in.

"That's right." Galen's face relaxed with Bates comment."You think fixing that road will be high on the list?"

Grady Hamilton lit his pipe with a kitchen match and scooted his chair closer to the table. He was the unofficial leader of this clan of sodbusters. Grady enjoyed their company, but he kept to ranching and feeding cattle. No plowing for Grady. The others wore seed hats that looked like they'd soaked in forty weight oil. Grady claimed his individuality by sporting a crisp Stetson. He had a deep, rich voice, and spoke slowly with authoritative conviction even when discussing something as simple as his wife canning peaches.

"If new money is coming to town," Grady said, "we should get the fairgrounds project back on the table. Everyone has talked about it off and on for years."

"The kids could use a 4-H barn with pens and a corral," Bates said.

"Exactly. If this town is going to receive money for community improvements, then we need a fairground."

"And an arena with bleachers where we could hold rodeos," Galen said. "You talking about that government track up north, Grady?"

Grady took a few puffs on his pipe. "Well, that land is too rocky to cultivate, and it's flat. But there are parcels of land available much closer to town, and we'd only need ten to fifteen acres."

Now that he'd brought it up, Galen pursued the topic of the abandoned government land. "You know, I'd still like to know why the government doesn't sell that land. Someone could graze cattle on it at the very least. Has anyone heard anything new?"

The other men shook their heads and raised their coffee cups for refills.

"I agree," Grady said. "It's been nearly fifty years since they've used that land at all. The government has their set ways, I guess."

Andy walked in as Bob Michaels added his two cents to the discussion. Andy grabbed a chair from a nearby table and moved into place between Grady and Bates.

"Feeling any better?" Bates asked.

"Not really. I feel like I had a half dozen bowling balls dropped on my back. Guess my head will heal up okay."

"How about the damage?" Bates asked in a caring voice that, for an instant, made it sound as though everything would turn out all right.

Andy dropped his eyes and shook his head. "Only had insurance on the truck and trailer, and they didn't get damaged. I didn't have the move itself covered." His voice trailed off as the other men squirmed in their seats at the thought of facing a major loss without insurance.

These men understood what it meant to have significant dollars invested with the possibility of financial ruin facing them every day of the week. Once a crop was in the ground, a hundred different misfortunes could mean zero income for the year.

Grubs could eat the roots of newly sprouted seedlings the instant they germinated. Cutworms could chew off fresh sprouts as soon as they broke through the earth. A hundred varieties of weeds could choke a crop while grasshoppers and birds ate at the growing plants. If that wasn't enough, Mother Nature was willing to take up the slack. Floods and drought, wind and hail, tornadoes and late frost could kill a high yield crop weeks before harvest and men of the land had no choice but to get over it and start again.

Every one of them knew the difficulty of balancing the enormous risks they faced against the cost of protecting against every peril. Everyone at the table liked Andy. But every one of them was thankful it wasn't them that faced a significant loss without insurance.

None of them mentioned the Carson boy. It was more than any of them wanted to contemplate or stick in Andy's face when he already had enough troubles. The boy's dad worked at the local machine works. His mother was a homemaker. There was an older daughter about ten years old. No one mentioned the tragedy. Seemingly, no one wanted to think about it.

"You heard about the money coming to town?" Bates asked Andy.

"No, what money?"

"Government money, free money for town improvements, or so we've heard."

Andy glanced around at the others. His eyes brightened as his brain considered something besides his troubles. "When did this happen?"

Bates chuckled. "Well, we really don't know. That's just the latest scuttlebutt."

"Free money? You sure you guys haven't been drinking too much apple cider?"

"He doesn't like free money," Galen said.

"How much?" Andy asked.

"We're not sure," Bates replied.

"Free, huh? Have you ever heard, 'if something

sounds too good to be true, it probably is.'"

"I hear you, Andy," Grady said, but I'm damn sure not turning it down. If the feds want to spend money on Elmwater, I say, more power to them."

"If all this free money stuff turns out to be true, think guys, think." Andy's gaze went around the table, and he looked every man in the eye. "That means the feds want something out of us. What if they come in here and want to bury radioactive waste out on that military property. You know those limestone formations only go down about fifty feet. Below that and the soil gets contaminated, the water table is at risk."

"They wouldn't do that," Galen said. "You've been watching too many movies."

"Why not? Once they've hung paper all over town, they can come in and do whatever they want. I'm just saying, if all this is true, we'd better find out the whole story before we get caught in something that changes the whole town."

"Listen, Branson; nobody needs to be taking any orders from you." Galen's voice had risen in volume, and his face was again red as a beet. Andy's whining had caught in his craw. He and the others had been having a spirited discussion of pipe dreams and money trees. "Maybe you should mind your own business and try not to get anyone else hurt."

Andy's move was as quick as a cat. Coffee cups went flying as table legs ground against the floor. His hand grabbed Galen's shirt in a vice, as a knuckle hit his throat, and he pulled the older man from his seat. "Take it back, or I'll flatten your face."

"Whoa," Bates bellowed.

Grady grabbed Andy's shoulders.

Galen could only cough, his eyes wide in terror. He raised his hands in surrender.

Andy relaxed his grip.

"I didn't mean it like that," Galen sputtered. "I'm sorry I said anything."

Andy let him go. Galen fell back in his chair. Andy starred him down for a second, then he turned, and walked quickly from the diner.

What had he done? Galen and his dad had been good friends and helped each other out numerous times. His fist remained clenched. His pounding heart gave way to heavy breathing, and he thought he might faint. He walked to his truck, ashamed, confused, and surprised at what had come over him. His dad had been through tough times, too, and he never saw him take out his frustration on another person. He had never done that before either. He had to get a grip.

His intention when he left the house was to grab a cup of coffee, then go to the funeral home. Now, the reality of dead Taylor Carson had been thrown in his face. Going to the funeral home was the last thing he wanted to do. But because of what had just happened, he had to go.

Andy was nervous as he got out of his truck. It was still early. There were only a few vehicles parked around the building. He knew the funeral director, elderly Myron Edwards. He handled two or three bodies a month on average and filled his extra time as a veterinarian for small animals, particularly house pets. He had a license in both fields and had been a pillar of Elmwater for more than forty years.

Why was he here? He was going to make himself sadder and more remorseful than he already was. He knew how his dad would handle the situation. Sometimes the right thing to do is the hardest thing to do – but once done, it becomes apparent that it was the only thing to do. Andy entered the building. A melancholy requiem played softly through the speakers in the ceiling. What a horrible piece of music, Andy thought. Only makes a person feel worse. The lighting was dim, the place smelled of the impregnated dust embedded in the thick red velvet curtains. There were two viewing rooms, and one of them was open.

Andy signed his name in the guestbook. Ten pages of names were already in the book. He approached the small casket. Andy gazed into the flat, expressionless face of little Taylor, and his eyes welled up with tears. The emptiness that gripped his heart came from knowing how hard he had tried to save him. He racked his mind for what else he might have done. Some saw his effort as heroic, others saw it as an effort in futility — such a beautiful boy. He stood beside the casket for a good five minutes, then wiped his eyes with his sleeves and turned to leave.

Myron stood outside the door. Quietly he had watched a scene he had witnessed many times before. "Thank you for coming, Andy," he said and gave Andy a gentle pat on the shoulder as he passed.

CHAPTER SEVEN

O N THE OUTSKIRTS of Kansas City, Daniel Romme assembled a welding truck with a cutting torch, a mobile crane, a backhoe with a front-end loader, and two forty-foot cargo containers with a trailer to haul them. He owned the welding truck and rented the other items. He was ready to begin work. There was a promise of a big payday, not his only motivation for the project ahead, but his primary one.

One night, just after 9:00 p.m., a semi-trailer laden with a cargo container full of tools, lights, angle iron, and steel beams pulled from a deserted warehouse headed west. Romme was well rested and ready for the all-night, round-trip run. He had several bottles of water with him along with a 9mm pistol under the seat and an AR–15 in a gun rack below the rear window. When he hit the state highway in Kansas, he kept the rig moving at an even 65 miles per hour. He was in no hurry. Slow and steady, nothing suspicious.

The 18–wheeler slowed to a crawl as it made the turn off highway 24 and began the roll up Main Street. The time was 2:00 a.m. The town of Elmwater was sleeping. A dozen street lights and a half-moon lit the way. A yellow bulb burned outside the police station with the town's three police cars parked in front. Romme eased the truck through town making as little noise as possible. He was headed eight miles north of town to vacant Kansas prairie, an abandoned stretch of land owned by the U.S. military.

He had to drive the truck through town because an old farm road that came in from the northwest was unusable by heavy vehicles. The road had insufficient ditches for adequate runoff. Every drop of rain washed lateral erosions in the packed dirt. Potholes were everywhere. The road was too narrow, as well, for large trucks. Until the road could be widened and graded, equipment and supplies would have to be cautiously brought through town. He and his comrades had to be at work on their project right along with the work going on in town.

Cattle slept in huddled groups under trees. Every mile or so, Romme would pass a farmhouse with a barn and several outbuildings. The moon in the cloudless sky illuminated the land in a dazzling half-light. Through open truck windows, the night air was clean and crisp.

Five miles out, he passed the fork that led to the left and the unusable 'old back road.' Three miles further north, the road came to a dead end. A collapsed metal gate lay on a cattle guard. The land wasn't fenced. Only a single sign bolted on a rusty pole gave any notice about the property. Romme stepped from the truck and moved the gate aside. He shined his flashlight on the faded letters.

No TRESPASSING – PROPERTY OF THE UNITED STATES GOVERNMENT

He left the sign alone, climbed back into the cab, and slowly pulled ahead. The land was a vista of knee-high prairie grass with the occasional sighting of a bush or gnarled tree, deformed long ago by the ravages of an unobstructed wind. Precisely two miles further north, he turned east and drove six and a half miles to a limestone outcropping. He backed the trailer in behind the bluff and dropped the cargo container.

He went back the same way, pulled the broken gate over the cattle guard, and slipped through town pulling an empty trailer. It was 3:40 a.m. Romme smiled to himself. Early morning chores had not begun. Even the chickens were still roosting. He was unaware that Andy had been peering out his kitchen window in the first house he passed as he headed back into town.

Andy continued to have trouble sleeping. He was up at all hours, sleeping when he could. His body still hurt. As hard as he tried to fight it, his motivation remained in the dumps. He had been standing at the window a good fifteen minutes when the truck and trailer rolled south toward town. Where in the hell did a big truck like that come from? Andy thought.

When Romme reached the highway, he kicked the truck up to seventy miles an hour headed back to Kansas City. He had delivered a significant load of supplies to the site, but there was more to come. Soon, they would open the hole to see what, if anything, was in it.

Mendenhall would be pleased to know he completed the trip without incident. Romme and Mendenhall worked well together despite their varied backgrounds. Mendenhall appreciated his mechanical and construction skills. Mendenhall also knew he was good with a gun and not hesitant to use one. Romme remembered quite clearly the way they first met.

ROMME FIRST LAID EYES ON MENDENHALL at a street market in Kabul while serving in the U.S. Army. Mendenhall was wearing a loose robe with his head wrapped, but he was no Afghani. His blue eyes and light complexion were evidence of that. Romme stopped him. Until he knew who he was dealing with, he didn't play games. Orders from Central Command were "Stop and Challenge" anyone or anything out of the ordinary. This man fit that description.

"Where are you from?" Romme quickly slid behind Mendenhall and ran his free hand along his waist. His right hand held his rifle, muzzle down, finger firmly on the trigger guard. Mendenhall raised his hands slightly as Romme reached around and patted his chest. "Don't turn around."

"Easy soldier. I'm just buying food."

"Ah, you speak English. Why am I not surprised?"

"I'm German. I speak four languages."

"So why you dressed like a goat herder?" Romme didn't care how the man took the comment.

"I'm a Muslim," Mendenhall said resolutely. "I've been living here while trying to help this country get back on its feet."

"Hmm, so would you like to talk to my captain?"

"No. Have I done anything wrong?"

"Not that I can tell." Romme looked him up and down. "It's just that you're an odd sort. My squad doesn't see many foreigners dressed, like you if you know what I mean?"

"I'm taking care of my business, Sergeant Rome." Mendenhall looked at the name on Romme's fatigues.

"It's Ro—me."

"Yes, Sergeant Romme. I come here quite often. I'm not hard to find. You can ask for me at the mosque."

"Not so fast. I didn't say you could go. What is your business? How do you make a living?"

"I'm funded by a German charity. I work with the Afghan Interior Ministry and spend most of my time at the mosque."

"Let me see your papers," Romme said. The man had an Afghan ID and a card referencing an obscure German organization. "Gregory Mendenhall. Did I pronounce that correctly?"

"Yes, sergeant."

"Okay, you can go." Romme lowered his demanding tone. The two men's gaze focused on one another. For a moment, each man intently studied the other, and each man took notice of the other's penetrating stare. "You say you come to this market often?" Romme asked.

"Almost every day."

CHAPTER EIGHT

THERE WERE THREE public meeting places in Elmwater besides the town's five churches – the bowling alley, the senior center, and the city auditorium. Although the obvious choice for a town hall meeting, the auditorium could in no way accommodate all of the town's eighteen hundred plus residents, give or take a dozen. The interior of the building was little more than a basketball court with a stage at one end. Capacity was listed at nine hundred. Bleachers that ran up forty rows on one side of the court were the extent of the permanent seating. A call went out to every church and school for all available folding chairs. Some folks showed up with lawn chairs or stools. Most of the kids sat together in groups on the floor.

The parking lot was jam-packed with vehicles

overflowing for blocks down the streets. Matt White and his wife even drove their tractor to town because their Ford was out of commission. Every adult was given a form at the door:

AT THE CONCLUSION OF TONIGHT'S PRESENTATION, PLEASE INDICATE

YOUR PREFERENCE ON THE PROPOSAL – I
   IN FAVOR
   NOT IN FAVOR
   SIGNATURE

The auditorium quickly became standing room only. If streamers had been hung from the ceiling and a brass band performed on stage, the atmosphere could not have been more festive. Everyone knew something exciting was afoot. If something beneficial was coming to Elmwater, then everyone wanted in on the story. It wasn't long before the building couldn't handle the overflow. The fifteen-foot side doors, used during auto shows, were flung open wide to let those outside better hear the speaker. For a moment, a pulse of humanity tried to squeeze into the auditorium. But the place was packed, and several hundred people were left standing outside. In the chaotic bustle of humanity, the distribution of preference forms was dispensed with.

On stage, behind the curtain, Del was a mental frazzle. Mendenhall reviewed the specifics of the proposal with the three councilmen and informed them that if the citizens approved the plan, it would

CLIFFORD MORRIS

become official. Mendenhall assumed that Del would make the public address, but the man was an emotional wreck. Del kept asking irrelevant questions and displayed no indication he'd be forceful and definitive speaking to the public. Warren stepped up and accepted the task.

A sea of folding chairs creaked as people adjusted themselves and gawked around the room. Farmers straight from the fields wiped their red faces and looked about for places to throw away their paper cups filled with chew. Gerald and Mae Morgan visited with everyone around them, all customers, and wondered how the business would be affected at the grocery store. Children played tag among the chairs. Andy found a place to stand next to the wall at one end of the court. He didn't pay much attention to what was going on. He had plenty on his mind, but he knew he needed to attend. Maybe he would learn something where everything would make sense. Or perhaps, he'd remain defiant in his assertion it was all a con job.

At seven sharp, the three councilmen walked on stage. Del and Garrison took seats behind Warren as he stepped to the microphone.

"Good evening," Warren tapped the mic. The buzz of conversation that had swirled through the building seconds before stopped. Even the children sat still. Complete silence descended upon the crowd. A person might have thought Warren was about to lead the assembly in prayer.

"I'm pleased to announce that the federal government has selected Elmwater as a community to receive a grant to expand and modernize the town's infrastructure."

An eruption of cheers and applause ensued. No one knew what Warren's statement meant, but it sounded good. Words like federal grant and modernized had nice rings to them. Warren waited a bit, then waved his arms to get the crowd to quiet down.

"We'll be able to curb, gutter, and pave all of the residential streets that are currently dirt roads. Expansion of the senior center is high on the list as well as locating the library in a separate building. We can acquire land and build a brand new 4 – H barn with pens and corrals, and an arena with bleachers for Western playdays."

Again a spontaneous tumult of cheers engulfed the auditorium. The commotion built to a crescendo and remained there. Warren could do nothing but stand and watch until the celebration petered out of its own exhaustion.

"This community improvement program has a monetary limit, but we will have up to three years to complete the projects I just mentioned, and be able to consider others. We need everyone to agree to participate and contribute whenever there is a need for extra workforce or equipment that is available locally. Everyone needs to be involved.

"For those of you who have a form, please complete them and leave them at the front door on your way out. If you didn't get one, you can come by the city hall tomorrow and fill one out – one per family, and they need to be signed. Any suggestions you have for other projects can be left at the city hall, as well. We'll publish regular updates in the

Schooner. That's all for now. Everyone drive home safely."

Warren wasn't interested in taking questions, an exercise he knew would digress into endless jabber of unrelated topics. He turned off the microphone and walked from the stage with Del and Garrison at his heels.

ANDY WAS THE LAST PERSON to leave the parking lot. The back-slapping and glad-handing carried on for a good thirty minutes while hardly a vehicle moved. When they did, it was to a chorus of blaring horns. What was the real purpose behind this government largess? Warren hadn't explained much. Andy's friends and neighbors were acting like a herd of lemmings. No one was asking any serious questions. He knew what his father would say: The quality in the shortest supply in this world is common sense. If you have any, use it.

When he got home, his five-year-old black Labrador, Tipper, met him at the door of his truck. The dog was always with him around the farm. Tipper was an excellent hunting dog, too. Inside the house, Tipper ate from his bowl then curled up in his favorite spot under the living room coffee table.

With a single light on in the hall, Andy sat back in his worn recliner and tried to think. He sighed and touched the scabbed-over gash above his eye. Why was he living in this house alone? He had grown up in this place, but now it was quiet and dark. He still had baseball trophies from his teenage years in the back bedroom. You wanted to be a farmer; now you're a farmer, he thought. What else do you have to show for yourself? Farming and side work had kept him busy, and time got away. At age twenty-eight, he should have a family of his own by now. He should have a son and a daughter, maybe two boys and the oldest would be about ready for elementary school. Maybe this was his destiny. Everyone he knew readily accepted him as long as he agreed with the consensus. But for him to suggest anyone think twice about anything, all he got was blank stares and admonitions to be quiet.

Andy felt sure he wasn't the only one in town who found this sudden influx of money into Elmwater rather strange. But he hadn't heard any dissenting voices. Andy knew his neighbors as practical, down-to-earth people. It would take more than the Pied Piper of greed to lead them down a path of destruction, wouldn't it? Maybe not. Maybe the physicological euphoria of unearned wealth overpowered common sense. Everyone dreamed of winning the lottery. Maybe the intoxication of free money was too strong to resist, too seductive to reject, too exciting to miss.

To hell with them all. If this boondoggle were going to throw money at the town, he'd stand in line and get his share. It might be what he needed to get back on his feet. People might forget about his fiasco with the house. Might be jobs for the taking and he could keep busy every day. The section and a half of wheat the custom cutters harvested for him during the summer had his bank account just under $60,000. Andy needed most of that money to get through the winter, and he'd still have to borrow from the bank to plant next year's crop. With the fees, penalties, and potential lawsuits he faced, $60,000 didn't feel like a lot of money. Maybe he should get on the federal gravy train when it ran through town, and play along like the others.

But he knew he couldn't look the other way. He had to get answers. That's what his dad would do. Curiosity scratched at his brain and created resolve in his heart. All of his neighbors were doing backflips over this government proposal, and yet, no one had seen so much as a dime. Maybe he had let some of his best years get away, but he wasn't dead. He intended to find out what was behind all the talk, if not for the town, then for himself.

CHAPTER NINE

THE NEXT DAY, before the doors opened, a congregation of citizens waited to get into city hall to fill out their preference form. The line became a serpentine mass of humanity that ran around the building and down the sidewalk. Evelyn Keaton passed out forms as fast as she could. She listened to suggestions for additional projects that should receive high priority. Her office became a madhouse. Everyone had an idea. People talked over one another.

One guy wanted to build a zoo with bears, monkeys, and the like. Another wanted to build a city swimming pool. Evelyn tried to explain that a swimming pool wasn't the kind of project that the government would likely approve. But she reached her limit when another fellow suggested a museum to house antique farm equipment.

She found a large cardboard box, wrote SUGGESTIONS across it with a wide black marker, cut a slit in the top, and placed a pen and a pad beside it. From then on if anyone so much as uttered the word 'suggestion,' she looked toward the door and pointed emphatically at the box.

A FEW BLOCKS AWAY, Mendenhall entered The Farmers State Bank. Whitmire was up and out of his chair when Mendenhall came into his office, met him halfway across the room, and shook his hand profusely.

"I'd say everyone knows about your proposal now," Whitmire said with a feeble attempt at a smile.

"Oh yes," Mendenhall said. "We're able to proceed." He waited while Whitmire waddled back behind his desk. "We need you to account for all expenditures by the city. Before any checks are written, you need to receive a signed bill for the work completed. Here, I believe this will get everything started."

He handed Whitmire a check for ten million dollars. The signature on the check was machine stamped, the name undecipherable. Mendenhall had plenty of business checks from a bank in Virginia, and he would dispense funds when needed on a schedule of his choosing.

"I'll have additional deposits when you need them," Mendenhall said, "I'm headed to city hall next to see what projects the city is going to undertake first." With that, he walked out, leaving

Whitmire to embrace the check in his hand, going as far as to smell the paper on which it was written.

Outside the bank, Mendenhall took a deep breath of fresh air and drove to the courthouse. In the grand scheme of things, everything was moving along. He wanted this sleepy town of gullible country bumpkins to keep busy and be so grateful for their good luck that they'd be oblivious to anything else going on around them.

Del was at the courthouse, expecting him, with an even more obsequious handshake than Whitmire's. "You don't know what all this means to the community," Del said.

"Washington is dedicated to helping all communities, large and small." Mendenhall found Del's toadyish demeanor nauseating. "Get your highest priority projects underway as soon as possible. We don't require that you bid out the projects. Select the contractors you want and get started. I left funds at the bank earmarked for the city."

"We were thinking about paving all the streets on the . . ."

"That will be fine," Mendenhall interrupted. "You have my number if you have any major questions. I'm the person to talk to concerning all matters. But it's your town. I'm sure you and the other councilmen can handle the day to day concerns that may arise." Mendenhall looked Del square in the eyes, hoping he'd instilled some backbone in the old geezer, and that he'd get the ball rolling. "Any questions before I go?"

"No, not that I can think of. Everyone is quite

excited as you can imagine."

"I'm sure they are. That's what we like to hear. I'll be back on Monday, and I'll check with you then."

On his way out, Mendenhall picked up the completed preference sheets. He didn't need them, but he'd keep them for now. They were only props after all. Any fool knew how the townspeople would vote once they heard the proposal. He could hardly keep from laughing out loud — what a bunch of American hicks. Every one of them had been out in the sun too long.

MENDENHALL CONCEIVED THE NEW PLAN because the original idea to detonate nuclear devices indiscriminately at street level lacked maximum devastation. Mendenhall knew atomic bombs are more deadly when discharged in the air. Three key variables had to be met – -secret preparation, indefensible attack, and a specific rather than random targets. Some on the team initially balked at his plan, but Mendenhall remained steadfast. He alone was responsible for a successful outcome. He would make the final decisions on strategy, timing, and target. Killing ordinary people was a meaningless exercise. Americans weren't afraid of the mighty hand of Allah, only wary. Deaths alone would not achieve a decisive victory.

What had flying airplanes into the Twin Towers accomplished? The Americans had become more resolute. They had mounted an offensive of their own. The Americans were lazy, corrupt, hedonistic, and infidels. But they weren't cowards. It was the governing head that must be severed to defeat them.

Mendenhall showed each member of the team the soundness of his plan. One by one, they came on board. The responsibility for a successful attack was fully on his shoulders. One strike. One massive strike. The Americans would never know what hit them. To implement his plan would require time and seclusion. Even more, the attack had to be something new, something completely unexpected. The use of commercial airlines was out. They were guarded, searched, and inspected more than the inside of a prison. Even more, any attack from outside U.S. borders would be quickly detected before the weapon reached the American coastline. Mendenhall knew he had arrived at the right answer. A single, devastating strike must come from within the borders of the United States, and the vast, empty plains of Kansas was the perfect place from which to launch the attack.

CHAPTER TEN

I T WAS EARLY OCTOBER. The high school, 8-man football team, lost to Bridgedale 20 - 14 Friday night. Carson Taylor was laid to rest Saturday morning. The funeral was scheduled for the weekend so that all of his classmates and their parents could attend. Myron Edwards knew his little chapel could never hold all the mourners who would undoubtedly attend, so the service was moved to the Baptist church.

During the week, the Carson home was inundated with well-wishers and enough food to feed an army for a month. Taylor's father, usually an easy-going, talkative man was mute through it all. His full attention was directed toward his inconsolable wife.

Missy planned to attend. She bought a black

dress and a hat with a veil. Her presence might not be welcomed. She was not a long-term, truly accepted Elmwater resident. Many blamed her for the accident, especially those who were there and saw the mishap with their own eyes. Missy sat at the back of the sanctuary and kept her eyes lowered. It was a sad affair. Taylor's mother wailed through the entire service, and many of the boy's classmates wept silently into their parent's protective arms. Missy was relieved when it was over. But she was pleasantly surprised, and her attention redirected when she got home and received an invitation to a Sunday dinner.

THE NOON MEAL ON THE SECOND SUNDAY of each month was a special occasion at the Morgan dinner table as Mae prepared a feast fit for royalty. She and Gerald would invite a few young people from town to share in their epicurean bounty and neighborly hospitality. As owners of the grocery store, Mae had access to any food product or ingredient needed to prepare recipes from her famous cookbook. Her culinary skills were legendary. Her Sunday dinner invitations were sinfully coveted.

Gerald and Mae were in their fifties with no children or grandchildren on which to dote. Twenty years ago, their only son, a handsome, athletic boy died when he fell from a boat, cracked his head on the propeller housing, and drowned before anyone could rescue him.

For years since then, Mae invited young adults to her monthly Sunday dinner. Her only requirements were that her invitees were churchgoers and single. Several now married couples had first met over Mae's chicken and dumplings. She made no apologies for her matchmaking meddling and quickly beamed a motherly smile whenever accused.

Bill Grayson arrived right on time. Clean cut, mid-twenties, Bill was an insurance agent in town. A natural talker and a people person, Mae invited Bill often because of his relaxed style of initiating conversation. He hung his suit jacket on the coat rack and waved at Mae in the kitchen, then clasped Gerald's palm with two hands and shook it vigorously. He wore a short sleeve white shirt with a wide flower print tie that appeared to cover his entire chest.

"Afternoon, Mary," he said, as he approached the couch and shook her hand. Mary Simms nodded politely and extended her limp wrist. She was bundled in a neck to ankle fabric entirely too warm for the pleasant day. Her hay colored hair was pulled back across her temples and tied in a bun. She wasn't ugly; instead, she suffered the affliction of plainness. She worked in the Co-Op accounting department. When she spoke, she revealed an intelligent, well-informed young woman, but she was entirely too shy for her own good.

Soon the screen door rocked on its hinges as Jason Downs, the youngest officer on the six-man police force arrived with Andy, a last-minute replacement when Billy Conrady had to cancel. Mae had called Andy last night. At first, he declined. He said he wasn't up for a social get-together even if it included her home cooked food. Mae wasn't someone who took no for an answer, so with Jason's help, Andy showed up.

Sheila Reynolds arrived in a yellow print dress. Her bright eyes danced with a mischievous gleam. Having just turned twenty-five, Sheila wasn't what you'd call a beauty. Her nose appeared too large on an oval face. Her large white teeth bucked slightly through glossy lips. But the total package titillated Elmwater's eligible male contingent. She was pretty enough and charming, owing much to her bubbly personality. Both Bill and Jason met her at the door.

"Come and get it," Mae announced. Everyone clasped hands around the table as Gerald spoke oft repeated religious phrases into his lap. With 'amen' everyone unfolded their napkins and eyed the table's bounty. A knock came at the door. Mae's eyes alerted Gerald to get up, and a few seconds later, he ushered a demure young woman wearing a dark blue dress into the dining room.

"I'm so sorry I'm late. I don't know how, but I got turned around trying to find your address."

"Don't give it another thought, dear. Please have a seat," Mae coaxed in a warm, gentle tone. "Everyone, this is Missy Eckles."

"Yes, that's me." Missy tried to smile and nodded around the table in an attempt to make eye contact with everyone. When her eyes came upon one face, her pleasant expression fell. She averted her eyes and took a drink of water.

"Okay now, everyone eat while the food's hot. Serve yourself and pass to the left." The main dish was a five-pound ham plugged with cloves, sprinkled with cinnamon, and basted in a candy glaze. There were two salads to chose from, four vegetable selections, and Mae's hot rolls made from scratch.

"What do you all think about Elmwater's good fortune with this federal project?" Bill asked after washing down a forkful of mashed potatoes with Mae's sun-brewed ice tea.

"I believe it's truly a blessing," Gerald said as he laid his silverware across his plate and addressed the group. "There are so many towns like ours, good, substantial communities where people want to live and raise their kids. But there's no growth. Without new people coming to town a community stagnates. There's no increase in population, so there's never enough tax money to make meaningful improvements. Kids move on as soon as they graduate from high school. Mae and I have been around a while, and without growth, Elmwater will lose everything that makes a town worth calling home. From what I've heard from Del and Whitmire we've been truly blessed. It's a great day for Elmwater and a great day for all of you. You'll be the ones who'll benefit."

"The Co-Op is considering requesting the building of another grain elevator," Mary said. "We only have four, two for wheat and two for corn. The milo crop keeps getting bigger and bigger, and it's all stored in metal buildings on the ground."

"The school district is going to receive enough money to buy new computers," Missy chimed in as she glanced again around the table. Her gaze hung a moment on Andy. He didn't look up. As far as she could tell, he hadn't even looked her way. There he sat, feeding his face, oblivious to the conversation. She had grown curious about him. Now she was slightly offended. He appeared to have shaved, but the only comb his blond hair knew was the wind and his fingers. His hands were big and rough. His face deeply tanned. Missy satisfied her lingering questions about this typical farm boy with the assumption he wasn't that smart or insightful. It was beneath her to be offended.

"Sounds great to me," Jason said as he reached for the gravy. "The Chief's going to request new communications equipment for the station, first thing."

"What do you think of it all, Andy?" Mae asked.

"Huh? Well, don't know. Guess I haven't decided."

"Don't know?" Bill laughed. "Don't know if you like holding a golden goose?"

At that, Andy sat up and wiped his mouth. "I didn't say I didn't like progress. I'm just not interested in being part of a dog and pony show.

"Why would the government select Elmwater for special money? We don't have an employment or crime problem. The schools are pretty good the way they are. There's no epidemics or people who can't get medical attention when they need it. I live on a dirt road, and just about everyone has a truck. You going to tell me the government's worried about a few city streets not being paved?"

As he spoke, Andy looked around the table. His gaze fell upon an unfamiliar face. Maybe he'd seen her before, but he couldn't place it. Immediately he sensed an elegance about her. She was modest and reserved in the way she sat. Tiny features on an angel's face. She appeared as a fawn, vulnerable and defenseless in a hostile world. But something told him that she was more than able to take care of herself. What was her name again? He hadn't been listening to Mae's introduction. He lost his train of thought for a moment until he realized everyone was looking at him, everyone but her. He cleared his throat and continued. "I've been thinking about this quite a bit, especially since the town meeting. I'd say there's got to be a catch. When does the government ever do something and not want something in return?"

"Oh, you're being silly, Andy," Sheila said. "Of course it's good news."

"Don't go spreading ideas like that, Andy," Gerald said, his eyebrows knitted, his expression disapproving. "People don't want to hear that kind of talk."

"You're not going to make any friends by looking for reasons to blow up a good thing," Bill said. "You should keep your opinions to yourself."

"Well, Mrs. Akers asked for my opinion. It doesn't hurt to question things."

"I'm just saying, you want to make friends, you play along with this," Bill said. "From what's happened lately, Andy, you need all the friends you can get."

Andy's eyes lit with fury. He was able to hold his tongue, but his expression and body language were unmistakable.

"Come on, guys. Cool down." Jason stood and

wiped his chin with one of Mae's fine cloth napkins. "I have to run like I said, I have to cover for Bradford at the station this afternoon. It was a delicious dinner. Thank you so much." Jason headed for the door. "You coming, Andy?"

Andy hesitated. He took a final gulp of tea. He wanted to stay, but his feet were moving.

"I can give you a ride if you want to stay for a while," Gerald said.

"No, that's okay. I probably should go." He continued after Jason to the door. "The food was great. Thank you very much." They'll never invite me to another Sunday dinner, he thought. And I don't even know her name.

ALL THE WHILE, MISSY LISTENED. The young man wearing the wide tie referred to an episode she wished to forget. She dropped her head and twisted her napkin in her lap. She would never be able to quit hearing about the loss of Taylor Carson as long as she hung around this town. The school board would find a way to drop her as soon as possible, probably over the Christmas break. They'd have to pay her for a full year, but they wouldn't have to deal with the political pressure of having her around.

Moving back to Wichita wasn't an exciting option. She had grown up there, gone to school there, but she didn't want to live there any longer. Missy liked Elmwater better than the prominent city of Wichita. She had accepted the Elmwater teaching job right out of college with all the excitement and anticipation of beginning a career working with children. She was close enough to stay in touch with family, but out on her own. That was exactly how she wanted it. Now her future was completely unknown.

But another thought vied for center stage in her mind. This man she thoroughly despised twenty minutes ago was not your typical sodbuster with more dirt under his fingernails than lucid thoughts in his brain. He spoke his mind and expressed it well. He was rough around the edges and aggravatingly untactful, but then, he too had been in an extremely stressful situation when they first met. Maybe she would see him again and get the chance to know him better. Missy decided she was in no hurry to leave Elmwater. Maybe she could get another job around town once the school board let her go. At that moment, Missy decided she would stay in Elmwater as long as she could.

CHAPTER ELEVEN

A WEEK LATER, a caravan of men and equipment headed back to the vacant stretch of land north of Elmwater, Kansas. The night sky was overcast. The moonlight flickered in a wave of lambency. Romme drove lead in a welding truck with another worker in the passenger seat. A backhoe followed chained to a short bed trailer, and a panel truck with equipment and supplies.

They came in from the north, down the bumpy 'old back road.' Romme was concerned about the trailer carrying the backhoe as it slowly rolled through the potholes. Romme hated taking the old road, but they had too many vehicles and too much equipment to drive straight north through town. They couldn't be observed driving across the private military land. It was worth a little extra time to maintain secrecy.

He led the vehicles east when he came to a particular dead tree that marked the spot to leave the road and headed across the virgin prairie. There were six of them in total. Three were Hispanic. They had experience in the oil fields and knew how to handle the machinery. They spoke little English and asked no questions. The other two were Arabs, spoke English, and didn't have to ask questions. They knew the plan as well as Romme. Six and a half miles later, they stopped near the cargo container partially hidden by a limestone bluff Romme had delivered earlier.

"It's over here," Romme motioned with his flashlight and led the way. A steel cover fifty-five feet in diameter lay partially hidden under years of dirt, leaves and dead grass. "Let's set up the torch and burn some of this off."

Once cleared, it looked like a manhole cover, a steel lid, massive in size. Over a hundred bolts secured it. Unscrewing them would be impossible. They unloaded a generator and a string of lights from the panel truck, and the backhoe from the trailer. The gas-powered generator filled the night air with a steady hum. "Aim the lights that way," Romme directed as he pointed away from the town. The Mexicans began cutting the nuts from the bolts with the torch.

The men faced an immediate problem once they cut the nuts from the bolts. The steel plate sat on the sheared bolts. No way would it slide off. They would have to use the front end loader to lift and flip the steel plate over. Romme jumped on the tractor and fired it up.

He inched the teeth of the scoop under the lip of the plate, gave the machine more gas, and with a crunch of grinding metal jerked the plate up off the bolts on one side. With the neck of the loader extended, he inched the tractor forward, and the bucket went under more of the plate. The plate lifted off the sheared bolts popping and grinding as each one relinquished its grip. Romme floored the gas to keep the engine from stalling. The weight of the plate was enormous.

Romme put the tractor in the park position as he could no longer move forward. The front wheels of the tractor were within two feet of the massive hole. As the plate rose, it could be seen to be a good two inches thick. The neck of the bucket became fully extended. It couldn't lift the plate any higher. The neck wasn't long enough to flip the plate over. Four feet in the air a horrible grating sound began as the teeth on the bucket lost their grip. The bucket scratched loose from the underside of the plate. A mighty whoosh of air accompanied a wrenching bang as the plate crashed back over the hole. The machine shuddered violently from the sudden loss of the weight at the end of the bucket, and the men darted from the hole as fast as they could move.

The sheer size and explosiveness of the plate banging against the bolts caused the men to take a few minutes to gather their wits. When it settled, the plate had wrenched itself off the bolts. If it could be dragged off without snagging a bolt, half of the morning's work would be complete.

"Run two chains through the holes, one about here and one here," Romme said. "Back up the two trucks and hook'um up. I'll keep the tractor over here in case I need to lift it again."

The welding and panel truck pulled together. The plate slid grudgingly across the bolts and off of the opening. Both vehicles pulled in low gear. Once in the grass, they dragged the plate fifty feet away. The string of lights was taken off the pole and let into the hole. The men leaned over to peer into the abyss. The smell of mildew and polluted swamp water hit them in the face. It was expected that groundwater would have seeped into the hole.

"The silo's 175 feet deep," Romme said. "Let's lower the tape and see how high the water is."

First, they lowered the lights as far as they would go. The lights passed a visible side passageway and kept descending. The silo was bored as a round hole. But with all the piping, ventilation handlers, electrical conduit and workstations the completed missile silo was a criss-cross mesh of girders set against the four walls in the form of a vertical steel box open at the top. They lowered a rope with one-foot markings. When they ran out the full 120 feet of line and hadn't hit the water, Romme was relieved.

"Good," Romme said. "We won't have to deal with the water. The lowest level of the substructure for the blast platform will begin at a depth of 100 feet."

He looked toward the town. All was dark and quiet. He gathered the Arabs to his side. "I'm staying in town. Pull the tractor behind the bluff alongside the cargo container. Pack up everything else and go back the way we came in."

So far, success. Mendenhall was right. A hole already dug in the ground for our use. A sixty-year-old abandoned Altas missile silo that would be perfect for their purpose. No one would suspect a thing. If questions came up, they were erecting a telecommunications tower. Another project to go along with capital improvements in town. Total secrecy. Complete seclusion. They could assemble the rocket, and no one would see a thing.

TEN DAYS AFTER THE SUNDAY DINNER, Andy could stand the wait no longer. He made an evening phone call to the Morgan residence. Mae answered.

"Good evening, Mrs. Morgan. This is Andy. I wanted to call and tell you how much I enjoyed your Sunday meal. It was delicious, and I should have stayed for more. I'm sorry I left so quickly. I should have stuck around."

"I'm sorry you left, too. You missed out on dessert. I baked three different pies."

"Well, I wanted you to know I appreciated the invitation."

"You're welcome, Andy."

"I hope you'll invite me again sometime."

"I imagine that can be arranged."

"By the way, I was wondering if you remembered the name of the girl sitting at the far end of the table beside your husband?"

"I'm not sure. I could probably look it up."

"Does she live here in town?"

"I think she was visiting a relative," Mae said.

"Oh?" A noticeable inflection of disappointment overtook Andy's voice. "I don't suppose you have a phone number for her?"

"Maybe around here someplace. I have so many papers on my desk." By now, Mae had a wide smile on her face and a gleam in her eyes as she playfully answered Andy's questions. "You know, now that I think about it, she was asking about you."

"Really? Oh, she probably asked about Jason, too."

"No, just you."

"Do you remember what she asked?"

"Oh, I think they were rather general questions, but I guess you caught her eye."

"You think so? Wow. It sure would be nice to meet her."

"Here, I have it. Her name is Missy Eckles." Mae didn't have to look up anything, except her phone number in her address book. "She's a school teacher. This is her first year in town."

"Guess that's why I haven't seen her around."

"Maybe," Mae replied. "I bet she'd like to meet more people around town. Did you say you wanted her phone number?"

"Do you have it?"

"Here it is," and Mae gave him the number.

"Thank you so much, Mrs. Morgan. I appreciate it."

"You're more than welcome, Andy. Goodbye."

Chapter Twelve

TAMMAN HANANIA ASSUMED HIS ASSIGNED TASK with the same meticulous dedication to detail evidenced throughout his career. He needed to build a rocket engine that would carry a total weight of 32 tons, 1250 nautical miles. The exhaust burn would be approximately 2 minutes. The flight time to the target would be less than 12 1/2 minutes. At burn out the missile would be traveling better than 2 miles per second, with the final leg to the target achieved by momentum and gravity.

He would build a solid fuel engine, and he would test its power. Secrecy could not be guaranteed while testing, but it was imperative to do so. There would be but one opportunity for the launch to succeed. The rocket had to carry the payload close to the target. By observing how much burn he got per foot of solid fuel, he could calculate how long the engine needed to be to achieve the burn necessary to put the bomb into the proper trajectory.

He and another Muslim named Raghib broke into an inventory yard and stole three 30-foot sections of PVC sewer pipe five feet in diameter with 1/2-inch walls. Back at his farm outside of Wichita, they used a band saw to cut the pipe into six, 15- foot lengths. They wrapped the tubes in 3/8-inch stainless steel using epoxy to stick the rolled steel to the pipe. Extra metal was extended beyond the ends of each tube and beveled outward at the ends of each pipe. Holes were drilled in the beveled ends to insert locking clamps and seals for later assembly.

They dug a hole in the floor of his barn five feet deep and slightly larger than the diameter of the pipe. They placed a board at the bottom of the hole as a stopper, and raised a section of pipe vertically with an overhead crane and dropped it into the hole.

Using a portable cement mixer, Hanania prepared a mixture of 40% ammonium perchlorate, 50% powdered aluminum, and 10% synthetic rubber. To this, he added enough water to mix the ingredients into a flowing paste. As the mixer turned at a slow speed, he placed a torch under it to evaporate off the water.

A smaller pipe, four inches in diameter, was inserted in the center of the standing pipe. The mixture, the consistency of warm taffy, was poured around it until, one by one, they filled all six sections with fuel. It took two hours for each section to set before the fuel mixture was hard enough to keep its shape but soft enough to allow for the removal of the smaller center pipe.

The sixth and last section had first to be fitted with fins before filling it with fuel. From a 1/2-inch thick sheet of heat-resistant aluminum alloy 6061-T6, Hanania and Raghib used a torch to cut four fins 84 inches high (seven feet) to attach to the rocket frame and bevel outward to 60 inches (five feet) at the base. Each fin was glued with industrial epoxy onto aluminum skin and secured from the inside with six bolts each into the 1/2 inch width of the fin. It was then set upside down in the hole, filled with the fuel mixture, and allowed to cool. It took the men five days to complete this phase of the work. The easy part was over.

Hanania was not a complicated man. He enjoyed living in America and adopted it as his home. He completed graduate work at the University of Kansas after his engineering studies at the Institute in Oman. He went to work for Boeing in Wichita on a state department granted work permit and worked there for twenty-eight years until the plant closed in 2014.

Hanania enjoyed America's well-stocked grocery shelves and modern car dealer showrooms. However, the echoes of a strict upbringing never left his thinking. He saw America as a cesspool of secularism. He never got used to the scanty dress of American women, the shameful flaunting of their bodies and sexuality. His wife had a job, but she was required either to be at work or at home. She always wore a scarf over her head and a dress down to her ankles. The very idea of the feminist movement had Hanania seething. How was it allowed for a woman to dispute the orders of her husband? Why were women permitted to march in protest to the authority of men?

He met Mendenhall quite accidentally on-line while he casually perused Islamist websites. Their relationship grew over many months. When Mendenhall learned of his area of expertise, he instantly had more than a passing interest in the man. But Hanania was not initially a fanatic. He was devout but slow to anger. He knew and liked many Americans.

Mendenhall kept after him. The cause of Allah needed him. He need not be a martyr, and yet, he could reap the blessings of furthering the faith. Slowly, religious zeal took hold of him. It was comforting and exciting to be part of a group dedicated to the name of Allah. By applying his knowledge, he could advance the faith, and in the process, guarantee his place in paradise.

Hanania understood jet propulsion as well as pilots understand airspeed. Jet propulsion required oxygen to operate, whereas solid engine rockets did not. Nevertheless, there were many similarities. Hanania could get a good idea of the power of the thrust impulse by timing the duration of burn and knowing the amount of fuel used in that burn. He needed to test one of the fifteen-foot engine sections.

After the fuel was completely dry, each fifteen-foot rocket section weighed 12,000 lbs, 66 2/3 pounds of fuel per inch. The purpose of the center hole in the fuel was to allow the entire engine to burn simultaneously once ignited rather than burning from back to front. This configuration created more power and reduced the likelihood of hot spots in the airframe. The fuel would burn evenly from the inside out.

His greatest challenge now was getting back into the old Boeing property, building #36 to be exact. Ever since the last aircraft, an E-4B built for the National Command Authority flew from the Boeing airfield, the place had been empty. Eventually, the facility found a buyer, but new uses for all of the real estate would take time to implement.

The idea of sticking a gun to the head of a night watchman and making him open the gate had crossed Hanania's mind. But maybe it would be best to conduct the test during the daytime. Hanania knew all of the test equipment would be gone, but the test platform would still be there. And the way it was configured, the light from the burning rocket plume would not show outside the building. There would be the roar of the engine, however, and plenty of smoke. Rather than chance the roar would wake people up from their sleep, it might be best to go about it during the day. There was a good chance that no one would give the noise and smoke a second thought as it occurred with great regularity from that location in years past.

With the help of a powerful hydraulic lift, the two men loaded one fifteen foot section of an engine into a Bobcat. In another truck, they loaded a truck battery, and a DeLaval type exhaust nozzle that would be attached to the rocket engine once it was on the test platform in a horizontal position.

For three days, Hanania and Raghib cased the perimeter of the plant. They saw no more than two security cars around the place at any one time, each with a single occupant. Much of the time, the guards were either napping in their cars or parked together chatting through their driver's side windows. Occasionally one of the vehicles would make a lazy tour around the complex. The morning shift came on at 7 a.m. Hanania and Raghib would drive up shortly after that.

In the two Bobcat trucks, the men each approached a different gate. Hanania went to the nearest Building #36. A few blasts on the horn brought a security car headed his way. He stepped out of the cab and waited.

The security guard rolled down his window and leaned his arm on the door. "How can I help you?"

"Here to pick up a thermal transducer from Building #36."

The guard looked at him as though he'd spoken a foreign language.

"Here," Hanania said. He showed the guard his old Boeing ID badge. "It's not a big item, but it's heavy. I have a lift in the back."

The guard opened his door and stepped out. He was a young fellow, probably mid-twenties, tall, and lean. "I don't know what you're talking about, mister. Nobody goes in there. Boeing's got nothing to do with this place now."

"Oh, I wasn't told that. Should have picked it up long ago, I suppose." As he finished speaking another security car pulled up followed by Raghib in the other truck.

"Maybe he knows," Hanania said.

"He doesn't know any more than I do. We don't even have keys to these gates, mister. I think you'd better leave."

"Ask him, will you? We notified your company that we'd be coming."

As soon as the guard turned, Hanania reached into the plastic lined ammo pouch on his thigh and pulled out a chloroform laced cloth.

"Frank, watch out," yelled the other guard, but it was too late. Both guards were head locked and put to sleep before they could put up a fight.

"Let's get them in your truck and tie them up." As soon as the two guards were out of sight, Hanania grabbed the bolt cutters and busted the chains that held the gate. They drove inside the property, closed the gate, and backed up their two trucks next to the building in a dock location hidden from the street.

The blast pad-testing platform was still in place, as Hanania expected. All equipment used to measure jet thrust was gone, which he also expected. But he would be able to watch and time the rate of burn. That would give him a close approximation as to how much weight the engine could lift and how far it could travel. He needed to be sure the fuel mixture he used would burn hot and fast. The faster the deflagration, the quicker the missile would attain the apex of its flight and the more power it would have to achieve distance.

With the motorized hydraulic lift, Hanania and Raghib picked up the rocket section and maneuvered it onto to the test platform. The engine lay horizontally. One end was against the wall. They strapped it down with eight brackets. The braces folded down from the wall and could be extended to accommodate and hold in place a cylinder of any diameter.

Raghib inserted ignition caps into the base of the engine and clamped cables to them that dangled to the floor. The cables were long, and he pulled them thirty feet to the side and set them beside the battery. The men then bolted on the nozzle. When the set-up was complete, there were ten feet between the base of the nozzle and the back exhaust wall. The configuration of the chamber turned at a ninety-degree angle and rose up against an eighty-foot chute to the outside.

Raghib checked outside the building for any visitors. He rubbed the 9mm in his waistband. If anyone showed up, it had better be the whole damn Wichita police force. If it were one or two curious snoopers, they'd be dead the moment they walked into the building.

"All clear," he said to Hanania.

Hanania gave Raghib a thumbs up, and Raghib connected one wire to the negative electrode. Hanania readied his stopwatch. Then Raghib clamped the cable clip over the positive pole.

A plume of smoke puffed from the engine, followed by a flash of light. In a millisecond, a blast of heat and flame exploded from the base of the rocket. A second later the building erupted with the roar of ten locomotives screaming down the rails. Instinctively, the men moved further back. The heat in the building became oppressive. The light was blinding. Smoke rolled and billowed up and out of the building. The thrust was immense and steady, the roar from the blast constant.

Then as quickly as it began, the entire wave of fire and heat abruptly cut off with a few dwindling tongues of flame. The engine had burned for one minute and fifty-six seconds. Fifteen feet of engine burned for 116 seconds. Five engine sections mounted end to end would burn the same length of time because the fuel would burn from the inside out, but would produce five times the thrust. Hanania was more than satisfied with the test.

Wild-eyed and breathless, the two men ran for the trucks. They abandoned everything they brought, including the exhaust nozzle. They had another nozzle in reserve. The two security guard cars were where they'd left them. No one stopped them. No one followed. They headed back to the farm by two different routes. Hanania's countenance was calm as he drove. But a pounding heart and adrenaline rush gave him a secret high, the unseen manifestation of his glorious sense of elation.

CHAPTER THIRTEEN

T HE HOSPITAL HAD BROKEN GROUND to build a new wing with eight more rooms and additional laboratory space. Trucks and graders were rolling into town to begin paving residential streets. Andy stopped by the diner before going job hunting. The place was almost empty. Only Grady and Bates huddled in the farmer's corner.

"Morning, guys," Andy said as he took his place and righted his coffee cup. Bates and Grady eyed him warily as he took his seat.

"What you got planned?" Bates asked.

"Headed to some of the work sites and see if anyone's hiring." The waitress came around and filled everyone's cup. Andy poured a stream of sugar into his coffee, then brought up what was on his mind. "You know, I'm glad the town is getting improvements. But don't you find it odd? I mean, I hear the city is going to buy land and build a 4-H barn. Are you going to tell me the federal government is concerned about something like that? Where is all the money coming from?"

Grady's expression changed immediately. "Why are you asking questions like that? I thought you got that out of your system when you jumped Galen."

"Look, he blamed me for what happened to the boy. I did all I could." Andy took a deep breath. "I admit I've been under a lot of pressure lately. I'll work it out. I'll make it up to Galen. But about the money. All I said was, isn't it odd? Elmwater isn't that big. We don't have social problems."

"Hells, bells, Branson. Why you got to stir up trouble? Whadda you care where the money comes from?"

Andy was shocked. He had never heard Grady talk that way, especially in that tone of voice. His slow, mellow way of speaking had gone up an octave.

"I'm not saying I'm against anything. I'm just asking a question. I can't believe no one else is curious about something like that."

"You're going to mess it up for everyone," Grady said. "I already got a cheap loan from Whitmire and bought feeder cattle to be delivered tomorrow morning – 300 of them. I can pasture them on my fallow ground, put two hundred pounds on them, and then take them to the stockyard to finish them out. At the rate the bank's charging, the carrying cost is next to nothing. I wish I had enough land to pasture 3,000 head."

Grady and Bates gaze held steady on Andy.

"He's right, Andy," Bates said. "You don't want to get people worried about something where there's nothing to worry about. Whatever the government is doing, they can't take away the improvements once they're completed. Let them fill out their forms and mark their charts."

"Leave well enough alone," Grady said. "Don't bring up questions to nobody. Don't worry about how the government people spend money. They spend money all the time." With that, Grady and Bates left the diner. Andy stared into his coffee cup and drummed his fingers on the table. His friends could sermonize all they wanted. Andy understood they didn't want the gravy train to end anytime soon. Still, there were legitimate questions to ask, and he wanted answers.

Andy drove to the auto dealership to see Buster Warren. If anyone knew what was going on, it was Warren. Andy was let into the office as soon as he arrived. Warren wasn't busy at the moment. He wasn't in the middle of closing a deal.

"Good morning, Andy. Haven't seen you in a while. What can I do for you?" Warren said as he stepped out from behind his desk and shook Andy's hand.

Andy smiled to himself. He liked Warren. But he could tell the warm and generous welcome, as though he was a soldier returned safely home from a foreign war, was because Warren thought he was there to buy a vehicle.

"I don't want to take up a bunch of your time, but

I was hoping you could help me out," Andy said.

"Well, sure, if I can." Warren's expression became all business. He sat back behind his desk.

"The town hall meeting, this government project business. How did this all come up?"

"They came to us. Told us Elmwater had won the lottery, so to speak."

"And what else?"

"What do you mean, what else?"

"Are they doing a survey?" Andy shrugged his shoulders. "Surely they want to see something specific accomplished?"

"Not that they mentioned, Andy. We're just at the beginning, so there's not much to tell," Warren said.

"Don't you find that odd? The government is making money available and not placing specific requirements on how the money's spent," Andy said.

"The initial deposits are in the bank. We know we have the funds for the top priority projects on the list. That tells me all I need to know."

"How much money will the town get in total?"

"I'm not at liberty to say." Warren stood and moved toward the door. "You're going to have to excuse me now, Andy. Give it some time, will you? I'll keep you posted."

Andy didn't like the brush off. Warren was too quick to dismiss him, too vague in his answers. Warren certainly knew more than he let on. This whole program was tied up in secrecy. Andy was going to do his damndest to untie the knots.

ROMME KNOCKED ON THE DOOR of Room #10 at the Prairie Trail's motel. Mendenhall was picking at a plate of Kabsa he'd prepared in the microwave. He put the plate on the dresser by the TV and sat on the edge of the bed.

"So how did it go?"

"We got it opened. Looks good, just like you said. Maybe fifty feet of water in it, but the blast platform will be higher than that. The crew's headed back to Kansas City for now."

"I've rented six rooms by the month, so the crew can begin staying here," Mendenhall said. "You can set up in room #9. You need to shave and change into shirt and slacks. We've got an appointment with the city councilmen at 11:00 a.m. I'm going to inform them of the good news – the town's new water tower. I'll tell them you're my assistant."

"I've made arrangements with an outfit in Topeka," Mendenhall said. "I gave them the specifications and told them to use blueprints for a tower they already have on file. They should start moving materials within the week. I told them the city would FedEx a down payment, so I'll get more funds over to the bank today."

"Okay, you want me to clean up for a meeting," Romme said, "but don't you think I should spend most of my time looking like a worker, getting around in the welding truck?"

"Yeah, that's probably best," Mendenhall replied. "Keep tabs on everything going on in town."

"That won't be a problem. I'll blend right in."

At eleven o'clock Mendenhall and Romme

walked into city hall. The two-story building was pushing a hundred years old. The white marble floor and steps appeared to be the only features where any attempt was made to make the building look regal and official. The wooden railings, wall paneling, and baseboards were all scarred, marked, and gouged. The council meeting room was furnished with an equally ugly table long enough to seat a dozen people with a similar number of straight-backed chairs.

Del, Warren, and Garrison were there along with another man who had a swath of freckles across the bridge of his nose and a shock of red hair. Del introduced him as Darrin Becker, general manager of the local Co-Op. Del welcomed Mendenhall and Romme and opened the meeting with a boring recap of the projects the city had undertaken to kick off the program.

"That sounds great," Mendenhall said trying not to reveal his utter disgust in this bunch of neutered lapdogs. Of course, everyone loves free stuff. He knew the more prolonged the charade, the more 'worthy and necessary projects' the townspeople would come up with. But then, that was the plan. Keep them busy. Keep them distracted.

"Mr. Becker would like to make a request," Del said.

"Yes, well, what can we do for you, Mr. Becker?" Mendenhall said.

"Thank you, gentlemen. You see, the Elmwater Co-Op has been operating for better than forty years with four elevators, two for corn and two for wheat. As you can see, this is farm country. The number of acres cultivated has steadily grown, and the kind of crops has become more diverse."

Romme spoke up. "The Co-Op is a private enterprise, isn't it?"

"Yes, but–the work we do serves the public good. I would compare it to, let's say, a boat repair company that works near a fishing fleet."

Mendenhall tried to act genuinely disheartened as he put his elbows on the table and interlocked his fingers under his chin. "I'm sorry, but large expenditures are for the city only. We are not authorized to approve private projects."

"The Co-Op can certainly pitch in a substantial portion of the costs," Becker said. "We're not asking for a handout, but rather a partnership. In fact, over time, the Co-Op could handle the entire cost. We need a bridge loan, you might say, some assistance financing the project over some time."

Mendenhall was about to put a lid on the topic when Romme leaned over and whispered in his ear. "Ask for a thirty-minute recess."

"Can we take a short recess?" Mendenhall asked. "Let us makes some phone calls."

"Certainly, if that's what you want," Del replied. "We'll reconvene at noon."

If Romme had something important to tell him, Mendenhall would listen. All they had to work with besides the money was loyalty to the cause and their determination to see things through. Mendenhall and Romme walked across the street to the city park. They were the only ones there. It was early November. The leaves were turning, but the days were still pleasant. They sat down at a concrete picnic table beside a giant pine. Mendenhall had the cell phone to his ear, pretending to make calls. The men sat on the same side of the table facing the tree.

"So what's so important?"

"You've been going to a lot of extra trouble to get a water tower built in town. Don't you have enough things to take care of without that? If that Co-Op handles the planning and pays for a good part of an elevator, you wouldn't have to deal with a lot of details of building a water tower.

"So what's your point? We still need – -oh yeah. How high do those things go?"

"Over a hundred feet. No bigger than this town is, that's all we need."

"Could they get it built in time?"

"They could if we gave them the go-ahead today, and they aren't called elevators for nothing. Once built, it'll have a lift that carries grain to the top." Romme grinned. "The very top."

Mendenhall pinched his upper lip and nodded ever so slowly as his mind examined Romme's suggestion. "I get your point. Very good." He cracked a smile. "Let's go tell those good-ole-boys we were able to pull a few strings. They can build their precious grain elevator after all."

CHAPTER FOURTEEN

I T HAD BEEN SEVERAL WEEKS since
Taylor Carson died. In that time, Missy could
have been a hermit living in a shack in the
woods for all the interaction she received from other
adults. One family wouldn't let their daughter return
to school until the girl was placed in another
homeroom. Missy knew many of the parents and
her colleagues were sympathetic to her plight, but
someone had to take the fall. There wasn't an
acceptable reason for Taylor's death.

The school board had three members, all with
children in school, all with ears to hear the constant
bickering and accusations concerning the school
teacher who let it happen. By the second week of
November, the board had found a replacement
teacher. The termination was immediate. The board

would pay her to the end of the calendar year. That was all. Her firing was for cause. If she wanted to contest her full-year contract, they would see her in court.

Missy had slept through another night of fitful nightmares as her dreams focused on the old house falling apart on top of her student. Her body begged for a good night's rest, but her brain constantly replayed the horror of that morning. The sight of Carson's bloody, dust-covered body when dragged from under the house remained etched in her memory. She was still in her nightgown at 11:00 a.m. on a Saturday when the phone rang.

"Hello."

"Is this Missy, Missy Eckles?"

"Who's calling?"

"This is Andy Branson. I was hoping to catch you at home this morning, and I guess I did."

"Who?"

"Andy Branson. I met you at the Morgan's dinner a few weeks back. Do you remember that?"

"I remember the dinner. You didn't say two words to me."

"That was certainly my fault. Things got a little hectic, and I had to leave so quickly."

Missy closed her eyes while the voice at the other end droned on. Her mind was still in a fog of self-pity. She wasn't in the mood for a caller.

"If you say so, I didn't notice," she said.

"Well, I got your number from Mrs. Morgan, and she said you asked about me so I thought I'd give you a call."

"What? I might have asked a question about that

odd little speech you gave, but that was it."

"Well, what I mean is, I was hoping you'd let me take you out to dinner. I certainly would like to do that."

A heavy silence hung in the telephone line.

"You want to take me out to dinner. Is that what you said?"

"Well, yes."

"Where? To the Dairy Queen for a basket of steak fingers? Does this one-horse town even have a decent place to order a meal?"

"We could drive over to Clay Center…"

"Oh, that would be great, another one stop light town and a Sonic Drive-In."

"I didn't mean to upset you. I'm sorry if I called at the wrong time."

"Oh, whatever. You'll have to excuse me. I'm not feeling well this morning." And with that, Missy hung up.

She lay on the couch with closed eyes, her fingers messaging her forehead. Someone had called to take her out, and she had been plain rude. And it was none other than that curious, over-bearing, fascinating, irritating, handsome in an odd sort of way farmer. She had little to do and too much time to think, and spent much of the weekend feeling sorry for herself.

But when Monday rolled around, Missy dressed as though it were another school day and drove downtown. She had nothing particular planned, but when she saw the ubiquitous Help Wanted signs, she changed her mind. There was a sign in almost every business window. Grayson Insurance displayed one in bright red letters. Probably for a receptionist, she thought. Not interested in that. The beauty salon needed a hairstylist, Warren Auto wanted salespeople, and the subcontractor at the fairgrounds was looking for carpenters.

She drove to the bank to make a withdrawal. Right inside the door was another sign, professional in appearance, more subtle perhaps, but a Help Wanted sign none-the-less.

FARMERS STATE BANK OF ELMWATER
EMPLOYMENT OPPORTUNITIES
SALARY AND BENEFITS

That wasn't all that was new. The place was bustling. Every available seat was occupied. Other folks stood around. There were only two tellers. Missy went to Ethel Aker's window, the head teller, and completed her transaction.

"Do you have an opening for new staff?" Missy asked.

Ethel starred at Missy for a moment. The older woman appeared frazzled and overworked. A silence hung between them for several seconds, and Missy wasn't sure she'd heard her request. "Are you applying for a job?" Ethal asked.

"Well, yes, yes, I guess I am."

Ethel's appraisal of Missy took all of two seconds. "Come back here, and I'll get you an application."

Once completed, Ethel ushered Missy into a side room. "We'll be right back, Bonnie," Ethel said to the other teller.

"You know how to count change, right? Mr. Whitmire needs my help. I'm going to hire you right now. I'll give you a cash box with $1,000 in it. Only accept checks written on this bank after you've checked the customer's account balance. If they're making a deposit, stamp their pink copy as a receipt. Bonnie will help you if you have any questions."

Missy's eyes grew wide as Ethel rushed through her orientation. She couldn't help but smile. She had no objections, but if she had, they would have fallen on deaf ears. Ethel was practically forcing her behind a teller window.

"We close at three. I'll introduce you to Mr. Whitmire then, and we can go over the bank's policies." Ethel pulled out a full cash drawer and stuck it under teller window #3.

"Welcome to the Farmers State Bank."

CONSTRUCTION ACTIVITY IN TOWN was in high gear, but Andy still didn't have an extra job. Maybe he wasn't trying hard enough to get on with one of the contractors in town. He couldn't get a job, couldn't get a date, probably couldn't even get arrested. He didn't quite know what to make of the rejection he received when he asked the school teacher out for dinner. He didn't ask many women out, and he was willing to chalk it up to her having a bad day. He didn't blame himself. Whatever her mood, he saw more in her than a daddy's girl who had to have her way. He would give her the benefit of the doubt, and he would call on her again. There was something about her he saw across Morgan's dinner table. He wanted to see her again and see her open up. He was well aware of his father's admonition never to quit. Besides, he had nothing to lose.

Andy had concerns about the source of Elmwater's bounty. Everyone said it came from the federal government, but he didn't see anyone around overseeing the expenditure of the funds or monitoring any of the construction. It didn't sound right to him in the beginning, and it didn't smell right to him now. He was watching for a clue. It was out there somewhere. He was looking for something out of the ordinary.

He was working in the shed when the postal carrier drove up.

"Got to sign for this one, Andy," the carrier said.

Andy went inside the house and read the return address on the envelope. It was from a lawyer in Junction City. With little doubt to its contents, he opened the envelope. It was notice of a lawsuit. The Thompsons were suing him for $250,000 for the loss of the house he had been entrusted with moving. He had fourteen days to respond to the notice.

"Why didn't they sue him for a million? Andy knew good and well, and so did the Thompsons, that the house wasn't worth any $250,000. Andy was sure they paid less than $50,000 for it. But he also realized, they weren't suing for the house as it existed, but for the house's value once they had it remodeled.

He didn't have money like that. The farm was worth more than a quarter of a million dollars, but what if he was forced to sell to pay such a judgment? Hollowness settled in his stomach. Even if he didn't have to sell the farm, he'd be paying on something like that for years. Now he'd have to hire a lawyer to boot.

CHAPTER FIFTEEN

R OMME MADE THE ROUNDABOUT trip from town around to the north fork of the rut-filled old road that went south, then east across the military land to the silo. He didn't want to make any trips directly north through town unless necessary. There were farmhouses on the road. Everyone who lived along there knew the road came to a dead end at the military boundary or forked onto that ungraded trail. Big trucks wouldn't go that way. Why would trucks be that far north anyway? He knew it was best to skirt the town and use that god-forsaken road even though he didn't want to when he and his men went to the silo. He wanted Mendenhall to insist that that back road be graded and graveled and the city should make it a high priority. They had discussed the road previously, but still, no work had begun.

He pulled his red welding truck near the cargo container and backhoe left at the site. Nothing appeared disturbed. No prying eyes had come around. He checked the cavernous hole; it was truly massive. A coyote or rabbit could easily mosey by and fall into the pit with no chance of escape.

His workers would return in three days. Their next project was a vast and critical undertaking. They had to build a blast floor halfway up the silo walls that could withstand 200,000 pounds of thrust impulse at takeoff. The cargo container held cylinders of acetylene, 500 feet of 5-inch steel I-beams, two rope and pulley work harnesses, and hundreds of welding rods. Romme was satisfied. Everything was in order, and he headed back to town the long way.

After he left the government property, Romme was a mile northwest of the dead tree marker on the treacherous old road when his left rear wheel slipped into a rut and the truck high centered. He tried to put the transmission in low and go in reverse. He tried gunning the engine to go forward. The wheel was in what amounted to a hole, and he wasn't going anywhere without help.

Romme headed on foot toward town. He had no intention of making this predicament a long, drawn-out affair. He would pay whatever was required to be back on his way. He stopped at the first farmhouse he saw. A farmer sat in the doorway of a shed petting a black dog.

"Afternoon, Romme said, I was hoping you

could help me."

The man stood and walked his way. "What do you need?"

"Got my truck stuck on the farm road," Romme pointed. Need some way to lift it and get the wheels back on the road."

"Yeah, that old road has trapped many a vehicle. I know someone who has a wrecker. I'll give him a call. "In the shed, Andy called Jake's Wrecker Service. "Jake said he'd be right out." They walked toward the house.

"Name's Andy." He extended his hand.

"The last name's Romme." They shook hands. "This'll be a big help."

"You're not from around here. One of the workers in town?"

"Yeah."

"I ask that because most folks around here don't mess with that road. You should just come in on the highway."

"Will from now on, I can tell you."

"So what project you working on?" Andy asked.

Romme hated the questions. He knew they were innocent enough, but each one picked at his facade of legitimacy. From the moment it happened, he knew getting the truck stuck was going to cause problems. He wasn't mad; he was nervous. Enough with the damn questions.

"Excuse me, will you. I have to call my boss." He punched at his phone and acted like there was someone on the other end of the line. "Found a man who called a wrecker. Should be able to get back on the road shortly."

"Well, come inside," Andy said. "Knowing Jake, he'll be a while."

Inside the house, Romme recognized the place for the bachelor pad it was. Hand tools and unopened mail covered the dining room table. The TV had a single recliner in front of it.

"You want something to drink? Water or iced tea?"

"You have a beer?"

"No beer," Andy said.

"Okay, water then." Romme walked into the living room. "Wow, these birds look fine."

Andy had two mounted pheasants sitting on shelves. Another, with wings spread as in flight, was on the opposite wall. Romme inspected them with keen interest. "You ever shoot wolves or coyotes?"

"No wolves around here. Plenty of coyotes, but I don't shoot them."

"Why not? They'd be fun to hunt."

"Coyotes are good to have around. They keep the rodent and jackrabbit populations in check."

"Humm. How about deer? Plenty of deer around here, I suspect?"

"Sure, but I haven't shot one in a long time. Deer are game animals. You have to have a license to hunt them in season."

"Bet I could get one in no time," Romme said. You ought to see my rifle. It's in the truck, an-AR - 15, extra-long barrel, thirty round magazine with a scope."

"Whoa," Andy said. "Why you got something like that?"

Romme beamed as he always did when discussing weaponry. "I'm Army. I spent two tours in Afganistan. It's a lot like what we carried there."

"You don't need something like that now though, do you?"

"Never know," Romme said. "Never know."

A knock came at the door. Jake had arrived. Romme rode with Jake and Andy followed. Jake backed in behind the welding truck and in no time, lifted it back into the middle of the road.

"Thanks a lot," Romme said. "What do I owe you?"

"Fifty dollars," Jake said. "Thanks for the call, Andy."

As Jake was leaving, Romme said, "You were a big help, too. How much do I owe you?"

"That's all right. It was nothing."

"No, really. Here's fifty for your trouble. Couldn't have gotten back on the road so quickly without your help."

Andy watched as the welding truck drove northwest away from town. The fellow had another eight miles to go before he hit the fork and the graded county road. He could easily get stuck again. But as Andy watched the clouds of dirt fade as the truck moved up the road, another thought crossed his mind. He appreciated getting fifty dollars for doing nothing. But the guy was in the wrong place, and he asked the wrong questions. Andy thought about what he'd been looking for – a cog that didn't quite fit the wheel. He would keep his eye on the man in the red welding truck. Something told him, he'd be seeing that truck again.

ROMME DROVE THE LONG WAY back to town and stopped in front of the motel. Mentally he kicked himself. He should have turned around with the wrecker's help and driven straight into town. Now, at least two people knew he was out there on the north side of town, and either one of them might start asking questions.

He wanted a beer. He wanted something to do in the idle hours of waiting until the next phase of the plan could proceed. He drove around the few square blocks that composed the bulk of downtown Elmwater. He saw a lot of activity going on at the Warren Auto Dealership. There was a small post office, the senior center, and a bowling alley. The town as a whole was a sad assortment of mismatched storefronts and hole-in-the-wall offices. Romme chuckled into the crux of his elbow and shook his head. What a bunch of sun-dried sodbusters. Did they even have a pool hall?

When he thought the best he could do was to get a soda at the grocery store and head back to the motel, Romme spied Fred's Tavern on the backside of the last block. He pulled his welding truck over to the side of the street and went inside. A couple of Coors signs hung from the walls, another over the pool table. A long neck fan attached to the twenty-foot ceiling slowly stirred the dust mites. The place smelled like it hadn't received a breath of fresh air since the day it was built. Two men played cards at one of the wooden tables as Romme walked to the back and stepped up to the bar.

"Coors draft," he said.

Fred grabbed a cold mug. He wore an undershirt and looked half asleep. Romme saw a cot in the back room and assumed the dump was both home and business. Without comment, Fred stuck the mug under the tap."

"Pull'er hard. It's mighty thirsty outside." Romme smiled.

"Dollar fifty."

"Here's two. Keep the change, Frank." Romme knew the name was Fred. He was trying to engage the man in a word or two.

Fred rang it up and said nothing.

Romme drank half of his beer in one gulp. "So what's with all this activity? Looks like something new being built all over town."

Fred shrugged his shoulders and took a seat behind the bar.

"How about you guys. It looks like there's a lot of money to be made around here."

The fellow closest to the bar turned. "Well, maybe there is, but right now we're busy." He drew out his words like he was talking to a three-year-old.

"Just asking. Just curious. Would think it's a hot topic."

The same guy turned back around. "Yeah but we're not the visitor's information bureau." Same condescending tone. He turned back to his partner, and they both chuckled.

Romme didn't have a quick temper. Patience, planning, and observation were all part of his subconscious deliberations when facing any challenge. Maybe the guy had had a few too many drinks. Perhaps he was the town smart ass. A minor insult was not going to get him all riled up. Too much was at stake. There were more significant objectives on the horizon.

But Daniel Romme was not someone to fool with. He was six feet tall and lanky. His hands were fast and lethal. Even with his lean build, he was amazingly strong. He was a killing machine in human form. These two prairie hicks should be glad he was thirsty.

Romme finished his beer and clunked the mug on the bar. "So, do either one of you know if there's an employment office in town."

The guy on the other side of the table piped up. "Look, mister, I'm the sheriff around here, and he's the mayor. If you have a question, you need to send us a memo, and we'll answer it when we damn well please." The two men looked at each other and chuckled again.

Romme decided to string these two goat herders along. Raise their blood pressure. Get them pissed off enough to eat nails, and leave before they got themselves hurt.

"I can tell you don't know much, but how about a place to get laid?" Romme paused long enough for the question to soak in. "But you two probably wouldn't know that either since you keep each other happy."

A lag time confirmed they were both dense as it took forever for the men to register the insult. The man on the far side was the first to move. His wooden chair ground against the cement floor, and he stood like his body was unfolding from a box.

"You being a wise ass, mister?"

"Did I say something?"

"Yeah, he thinks he's clever," said the other man, now standing as well.

"Listen, I appreciate you guys trying to help, but I can tell you two have to look at a card to remember your names. I have to go now. Things to do."

One man blocked his path to the front door. Romme took three steps, blocked a roundhouse fist, and kicked the guy in the groin all in one motion. All fight drained from the other man as his expression registered shock, and he knelt to help his friend.

"Have a nice day now." Romme returned to his truck, shrugging his shoulders and rotating his neck. Nothing like some lightweight sparring to relieve pent-up stress.

CHAPTER SIXTEEN

F ROM KARACHI, PAKISTAN, a two hundred ton freighter sailed west. The forty-day journey to America would make stops in Muscat, Oman, and Port Elizabeth, South Africa dropping off containers, picking up others.

Within the stacks were eight cargo containers of bales of Basmati brown rice. Within two bales, each in a different shipping container were two, fifty-five-pound slabs of U-235 uranium. Each of the four radioactive slabs measured 22" X 22", sealed in a glass enclosure, encased in lead, and resting in a bed of wild rice. The freighter moved at ten knots around the tip of Africa and across the ocean. On the vast Atlantic, the huge vessel cut through swells without any sense of motion. The air was hot in the lower latitudes. The days were long.

By the middle of November, the freighter reached the Port of Houston, Texas, USA. The ship moved through Galveston Bay up Buffalo Bayou to a familiar terminal and unloaded seventy containers full of various commodities. Eight railroad car containers of Pakistani rice now sat on a Houston dock.

After a short trip by truck to the nearby rail yards, the eight cargo containers were loaded on Kansas City Southern rail cars headed north. The train's destination was Chicago with stops at Dallas, Wichita, and then Kansas City, where the eight cars of rice left the train. Six were trucked directly to a nearby mill. The other two, with distinct markings, were transported to a secluded warehouse in North Kansas City.

Asim Maroun was at the warehouse. With the discipline of a military drill team, two forklift operators plus six additional men opened the side doors and removed bales until the specifically marked bales were located and removed from each container. They shuttled the marked crates into the warehouse. Cargo boxes filled with raw rice identical to the bales taken were replaced in the containers. Those containers were then trucked to the mill, too.

Now the delicate precision work in the warehouse would begin.

BAND CONCERTS IN THE PARK were a Friday evening tradition in Elmwater for longer than anyone could remember. They were a year-round event. When it got too cold, concerts were moved indoors to the city auditorium. But unless the wind was howling, or there was snow on the ground, the concerts were held in the park. This evening was pleasant. Nothing more than a sweater was needed to enjoy the outdoors. Families relaxed below giant oaks and pines that dotted the park. Off to the side, an ornate fountain spewed sheets of water over a concrete statue of a boy holding an umbrella.

Members of the Elmwater Prairie Band included anyone who had an instrument and wanted to join. The ensemble was decidedly rich in enthusiasm and short on talent. Mr. Barrows was the oldest living member – he'd been the high school band director back in the eighties. He was good for two, maybe three, numbers on his saxophone. After that, he would sit out the rest of the performance. Ronnie Shafer didn't have that problem. He could blow his tuba all night long.

After work, Missy went home to change clothes. She decided to walk to the park for the concert. She dressed comfortably in a white blouse, khaki trousers, and a sweater. The walk was relaxing, therapeutic; the cool dryness of the prairie falling into evening while an orange-red sun descended behind distant clouds. In August she attended the concerts with Rita Henshaw, another teacher. Now she went by herself. Rita had begun to drive to Salina every weekend to see a young man there.

The band played the 'Star Spangled Banner' roughly in the key of C. Their repertoire consisted mainly of marches and show tunes. The concert lasted until the band played through their entire, never-changing list of songs. But even more than the music, Missy came to see the people. Listening to the rise and fall of happy voices was more enjoyable than sitting at home watching TV. Missy sat on one of twenty wooden benches in a sea of picnic blankets and lawn chairs, running children, and scrambling mothers. Several of her second graders spied her and ran over to visit.

Across the street, Andy exited Rick's diner. The band blared the beginning of the national anthem. The notes filled the air and rolled crisply down the street with a familiar melody. He was in no hurry to go anywhere. He had eaten a leisurely supper and had planned to head home. But sounds from the park beckoned him. A chorus of locusts, invisible in the trees, sang their monotone accompaniment to the blare of the horns.

Andy's eyes focused on the stage as he crossed the street, climbed the knee-high stone wall, and walked along the lengthening shadows of the park's high trees. It wasn't until he stepped on a blanket Andy realized he'd walked in someone's way and now stood in front of many in the audience. The music and atmosphere had mesmerized his thoughts. Now he ducked, embarrassed, eyes searching for an escape.

"Come here," came a voice. "You can sit here." Andy shuffled toward the sound. "Johnny and Dalton, would you boys consider giving up your seats to this man?"

"Yes, ma'am," the boys replied in unison as they scampered away, snickering to each other as they fled.

Andy reached for the bench seat and quickly sat

down. "Thank you much. I wasn't watching where I was walking."

"I don't think you stepped on anyone," she said. "It's a beautiful evening to be in the park, don't you think?"

He answered a reflexive, "Yes, it is a beautiful evening." The falling dusk cast shadows across her face. "Do you come here often?" he asked.

"Just Friday evenings. To hear the band," she replied in total sincerity as though the question deserved a thoughtful answer.

"I hardly ever come, never thought of it much. Guess I've been missing out," Andy said. "I've had so many things on my mind lately. "

She looked at him closely. "You're Andy, right?"

"Do you know me?"

"Well, I know you called me the other day and asked me out to dinner."

The audience sat in deepening darkness. The only light illuminated the band on stage. "Missy?"

"That's me."

He turned and leaned closer. "Wow, I didn't know this was my lucky day. Your voice is as beautiful as you are."

She laughed lightly. "And you're quick to make up corny one-liners."

"Oh, I'm not making up anything." His words wrapped in sincerity were spoken to only her. The crowd around them were absent from his mind, and he took her hand. She jumped a little at first, but only a bit, just for a second.

"I know my big ole hand is rough, but I hope

you're not offended. Your hand is as delicate and soft as I imagined." He placed her hand back in her lap.

"So, you did notice me at the dinner?"

"Most certainly. I've wanted to talk to you since that day. I don't know why I left so soon."

Missy extended her arm and placed her soft fingers on top of his steady hand. They sat in silence, taking in the clean smells of the evening. They could have been on the fifty-yard line in Arrowhead Stadium with an overflowing crowd in the stands, and they would have been aware only of themselves. For the rest of the concert, they didn't move, content to be silent as the music floated by on the breeze.

When the concert was over, Andy turned and said, "I'd like to drive you home, but my truck is quite a mess."

"That's okay. I walked here anyway. I live over on Peach Street. Would you walk me home?"

They walked hand in hand. The street lights caught a fuller glimpse of her beauty. When Andy gazed into her eyes, he was smitten.

"Do you remember when we first met?" she asked.

"At the Morgan's Sunday dinner," he replied, thinking they had already established that.

"We met once before that," she said. Her head was down as they walked, her words stated matter-of-factly without any hint of judgment.

"Oh." He hesitated. "I though I might have seen you before, but I must admit, I don't remember where."

"When that old house broke apart in the street, and you had pulled the boy out from under it."

She stopped and turned to face him.

"Go on," he said.

"I approached your truck as you were about to leave and thanked you for risking yourself to save the boy."

"And I yelled and chewed you out." A silence hung between them. She didn't act upset or offended. Maybe she just wanted him to know. But Andy swallowed at the sudden flood of guilt that filled his chest. "I'm so sorry. I don't usually get that carried away. What can I do to make it up to you?"

She smiled and squeezed his hand a little tighter. "What you just did," she said. "Apology accepted." She smiled and looked into his eyes. It was as if he had known her for years. He knew he didn't need to explain himself further or exaggerate anything about himself or his past. In no time they were at her door.

"Will I see you again?" he asked.

She faced him and took his other hand as they stood on the sidewalk. "When would you like?"

"Would you like to go to a movie tomorrow night?"

"Yes."

"Great. I'll pick you up at 6:30. But before I go, I need something to tide me over."

Pleasant surprise colored her expression. "What's that?"

"I hope you won't consider me too forward, but..." He took his cue from the acceptance in her eyes and pulled her closer and kissed her on the cheek.

CHAPTER SEVENTEEN

THE NEXT DAY, ROMME SLEPT in. It was past eleven when he looked out his motel window. Mendenhall's car was in the lot. Mendenhall answered his door while eating a twisted roll, and his mouth was full. Except for sunlight peeking through beside the curtains, the room was dark.

"What is that?" Romme asked.

"Lunch," Mendenhall said, still chewing.

"We've got to get that back road fixed," Romme said. "It's the only way in and out of the site that will not attract attention."

Mendenhall ran his tongue around his teeth and dipped his roll in a bowl of sauce. Romme could tell Mendenhall was in one of his contemplative moods. He had no sense of urgency. Romme kneaded his face with his fingers, walked to the window, and pulled the curtains apart.

"Let's have some light." Romme plopped into the chair by the door.

Mendenhall was his superior in the grand scheme of things, but Romme wasn't keen on being ignored. He did his job, quality work, and on time. The condition of that back road ate at his craw. He needed Mendenhall to pull some strings, and he needed it now.

"I got stuck out there and had to get two locals to pull me out. If I can get stuck, the bigger trucks can have problems, and it's not a good idea to bring everything through town."

"Asim got his package." Mendenhall said as he patted his chin with a napkin oblivious to what Romme had said."

The news shifted Romme's thinking onto another wavelength. "Good – that's good."

"Asim will be busy for several weeks. There's plenty of time to get your road repaired."

"No," Romme was emphatic. "We have a lot of work to do. The men are coming back in two days. We need to be able to use that road now."

"Okay, okay," Mendenhall said. "I'll talk to the city council, and insist it's their highest priority."

Romme changed the subject. "Are you going to have enough money to last until the launch date? I mean, these townspeople are like hungry dogs after fresh steak since they've seen an outlay of money. The projects already underway are nothing compared to what they'll come up with next. They'll figure out a way to spend every dime you told them was available."

"Let me worry about the money. There's fifty million in the bank back east. That will go a long way."

"That grain elevator won't be cheap."

"Who gives a damn. I'll delay payments if I have to. We're not shelling out any more money than it takes to get to January 21st. You know that. Just relax."

"The bank has a line of people out the door every day. Did you tell that banker he could make personal loans?"

"Yes, but only small loans mainly for down payments on equipment or home improvements. I figured that would keep everyone happy and focused on their own little projects."

Romme smacked his fist into his other hand. "I have a feeling that banker is playing fast and loose with the cash. There's a lot of new trucks and cars rolling around town. Could be that banker thinks the well will never run dry and is passing out money for any reason to anyone with a pulse."

Mendenhall fell silent. He finished off a bottle of soda water and walked to the window. "You may be right," he said. "That banker and that councilman named Warren. I need to pay both of them another visit."

AT HANANIA'S FARM, the two security guards from the Boeing property were kept separated. Their hands and feet were bound, their eyes and ears covered. Late that night, they were taken in different cars by different routes back into Wichita. Each man was dropped off in a secluded location.

Raghib had the guard who Hanania had spoken to at the Boeing plant. He backed into a cemetery off of North Broadway and pulled the guard feet first from the backseat of the car. The guard smashed his head and shoulder against the stone pathway as he fell from the vehicle. "Count to a hundred before you get up," Raghib said. "If I see you in my rearview mirror, I'll come back and slit your throat." With that, he cut the cords binding the guard's wrists and drove away.

A half an hour later, the guard stumbled into an all-night convenience store. The clerks immediately knew he was in distress. His uniform was torn and dirty. The back of his head was bleeding. "Call the police," the guard said as he braced himself at the counter to remain standing.

A police squad car took him directly downtown. At the station, they bandaged his head. The guard was given a bottle of water as two detectives escorted him into a private room.

"How many were there?" asked one of them.

"At least two, maybe more."

"What did they want?" asked the other detective.

"They wanted in the gate. Said they were there to pick up something in Building 36."

"What were they, white, black, Asian?"

"I couldn't tell. White, I think, maybe Hispanic. One of them showed me an expired Boeing employee identification card. He tried to get me to take it as authorization to enter the place."

"So you got a name?"

"No, I didn't read it that close."

"So, where did they take you?"

"Don't know. It was somewhere nearby, but they had my eyes and ears covered the whole time."

The two detectives looked at one another. They knew they had nothing. "Okay," one of them said. "We'll get one of the officers to take you home."

It was a different story at the Boeing plant. When the guards went missing someone called the police. Once the authorities were in the plant, the Kansas Bureau of Investigation and the FBI were brought in, too. Everyone who entered couldn't believe what they saw. Someone fired a sizeable rocket engine. The blast pad was still warm. The sight provoked a hundred questions, the answers to which prompted a hundred more.

Who would go to all this trouble, and why? It was more than some enthusiasts test firing a model rocket. So what was the purpose of the test? The authorities collected everything not nailed down as potential evidence, including the battery, the cables, the lift, and the rocket engine and nozzle. The residue would be analyzed, and the fuel ingredients determined. A detailed assessment on every item found in the building would be made to see if anything could be traced back to where it was bought or made.

Every component of the rocket frame would be disassembled and undergo the same scrutiny. The FBI took command of the investigation. The Department of Homeland Security was informed. Investigators were in the building well into the night dusting for prints, searching for any and every possible clue.

BY NOW MOST PEOPLE who knew Andy were prone to dismiss his negative attitude about the government money as someone who didn't like the idea of others getting ahead. He'd always been headstrong. His opinions weren't accepted or appreciated by a good many people. Town folk kept their distance. It wasn't that they didn't like Andy; it was a matter of avoiding negativity. If Andy had ideas as to what was right for everyone else, he could tell them to his dog.

Andy made himself coffee and fried sausage patties cut from the roll. He'd already fed and watered eight feeder calves he was raising. Missy told him everyone was applying for loans at the bank. He needed to ask for one himself. With the legal bills he'd have and substantial judgments likely in the future, he needed a loan. He knew the loans were coming from the government money. Any stares he got when people saw him speaking to Whitmire were sour expressions he'd have to endure.

Dust billowed up the road as he stepped on his porch. It was the postal truck again. Andy got his regular mail at the post office. This delivery had to be another certified letter or package.

"Sign here for me, Andy."

Andy feared more bad news. The only good thing to happen to him in the past month was meeting Missy. He looked at the return address on the envelope. It was from the office of another attorney, this one in Topeka. He sat on the porch and opened it with the care of a condemned prisoner, eating his last meal.

The Carson's were suing him for Taylor's wrongful death for $100,000. A wave of debilitating regret ran through his body. The letter dredged up all the pain he'd endured in the days after the event. It was as though it happened again. He felt sorry for the family, and the realization he could do nothing to ease their hurt.

The lawsuit was an act of desperation on the part of the Carson family. It was a blind effort to bring back some normalcy, some semblance of the family life they had before. Even Andy knew that the death of a grade school boy who earned no income and supported no one would not garner a judgment anywhere near $100,000. It was a strike back at Andy to make him hurt as much as they did. If that was their intent, they were close to succeeding.

Andy drove around town for an hour reliving the struggle he and Taylor had under the collapsing house. Finally, he headed toward the bank. He wanted to see Missy. Just the sight of her would lift his spirits, and he needed to talk seriously to Whitmire about a loan. He could no longer act above it all when it came to the government largess. It would still be a loan, but the money was available. In his mind, the whole thing was still fishy, but until he could figure out what was going on, he had to get his piece of the action.

The bank lobby was indeed busier than usual. People were talking in small groups or reading magazines. Everyone was waiting.

Andy went to Missy's teller window and placed

both hands on the brass bars and leaned in close. "I've heard the prettiest girl in town works at this here bank," he whispered.

"Andy, don't." She smiled.

"Don't what, little lady?"

"Andy, you're embarrassing me. I'm working."

"See here, little lady, I'm not here to chit-chat. I'm here on business."

"I'm sure you are."

"I'm here to see Whitmire."

"Great. Take a number." She motioned toward the lobby.

"That's what I thought. So let me take you to lunch." He took his hands off the brass bars.

"Oh, Andy, I can't. We've been so busy we've been bringing in sack lunches. Come back at two. I'll get you in to see him."

"Thanks, Sweetie."

"And then you can take me to supper later."

"For sure, but . . . it'll have to be the diner."

"The diner will be fine, Andy."

He touched his hand to his mouth and blew her the softest kiss over the tops of his fingers. She blushed and dropped her eyes, but the hint of a smile never left her expression.

CHAPTER EIGHTEEN

WHEN ANDY RETURNED TO THE BANK, Missy took him to Whitmire's office. The banker didn't meet him at the door. He was seated with his elbows on his desk and appeared exhausted as if discussing financial transactions and pushing a pen constituted hard labor.

"No more customers today, Miss Eckles. Tell anyone still out there to come back tomorrow."

"The Trammel's are waiting. They have an appointment for two fifteen."

"Okay, I'll see them shortly. But no more today."

"Yes, Mr. Whitmire."

Whitmire pointed at a chair. "What can I do for you, Andy?"

"Doling out all this money keeping you busy, huh?"

Whitmire nodded and scratched his ear. "Helping folks out with some of the government money," he said.

"You need another loan officer."

"I've thought of that, but I like to handle bank business myself. How can I help you today?"

"Well, for one thing, I sure would like to know what this money is all about. I know, it's supposed to be for Elmwater improvements, but what does the government want in return?"

Whitmire gazed back at Andy like the question had no meaning. After a long pause, "I don't know that they want anything, Andy. You're making assumptions with no basis. It's a straightforward grant to improve the community."

"I don't believe it. Money always comes with strings attached, especially from the government. They either want your vote or an endorsement or, who knows, they may come in here after all the work is complete and want to build a prison on that old air base property. It might be good for business, but it would change the whole make up of the town. Why hasn't anyone got to the bottom of this 'free money'?"

Whitmire sat back and rubbed his face. "Look, Andy, if someone hands you a brand new hundred dollar bill are you going to ask what mint printed it? All this is just getting started. Everything relevant will come out in good time, and I think you're getting worked up about nothing. I can't tell you anything more than that, because I don't know anything more."

Andy took a deep breath and squeezed the arms of the chair. He couldn't believe all the gullible, blind lemmings this town had for leadership. "Well," he said."I need a personal loan, too."

"For what purpose?"

"What do you mean, for what purpose?" Because you have the money and everyone else is getting one. They are loans, aren't they? You're not just doling out government money?"

At first, Whitmire ignored the question. Then he moved in his chair, his voice raised. "Of course they're loans."

"Okay, for my business."

"Andy, be reasonable. You and everyone else knows your hauling business isn't going anywhere. And, I can't make any crop loans with this money, so I don't think I can help you."

"What? Are you kidding me? You don't have to conform to any strict guidelines, and I know it. Call it a home improvement. I need the loan."

"Maybe if you needed to buy farm equipment. I might be able to loan you funds for a down payment." Whitmire hesitated a moment. "Or if you wanted to buy a truck."

A truck? It was true: the Silverado he drove looked like it had endured mortar fire with all its dents and scratches. It had more than 150,000 miles on it, but it still ran fine. But Andy didn't come to the bank to finance a truck or any equipment for that matter.

Andy rose from the chair, walked to Whitmire's desk, and stretched his arms across it with his hands flat on two stacks of papers. "Make it for $30,000. I want a loan, and you have the money. You're going to make me a loan or I'm going to turn over every shady deal you've ever made." He watched Whitmire's eyes grow wide, and his face contort in an expression caught between anger and guilt.

"I can't loan you $30,000, Andy. There's not enough money available. I've been making small loans of five or ten thousand.

Andy starred him down for a good thirty seconds. Whitmire didn't say another word, though his eyes returned a fierce stare. Andy walked from the room, his teeth clenched. There he'd done it again. He probably screwed himself big-time with that bluff. But his instincts told him Whitmire was involved in plenty of shady deals. Trust your gut, his dad often said, and don't let people push you around. People may hate you, but if they know they can't push you around, you're much better off.

When Andy reached Missy's window, his face was relaxed. "I'll pick you up at 5:30."

"How did it go?" she asked.

"Perfect. Everything went fine."

MENDENHALL WAS TIRED of the dusty little town, barely a dot on the map. Back and forth to Kansas City. He holed up in the motel most of the time when in Elmwater. He brought food from Kansas City but went to the grocery store to pick through what they had when he ran short. Bought unfiltered Pall Mall cigarettes and thought they smoked like a turd rolled in toilet paper; longed for good Turkish tobacco. Purchased bottled water by the twelve pack and searched unsuccessfully for anything approaching strong tea.

He went to city hall in search of the mayor. Evelyn said Del was likely at his regular job at the farm implement dealership. Mendenhall found the grounds full of emerald green John Deere tractors, combines, planters, and spreaders, all in rows, cleaner and shinier than they would ever be again. Del was busy when he arrived. Mendenhall watched with increasing boredom the activity at the parts counter. He poured coffee into a styrofoam cup and drank it black.

Del ushered him into his office and shut the door.

"Good morning," Del gushed. "What brings you by?"

"I've been getting some inquiries about a project the council didn't put on your priority list. Since there are road graders and pavers in town, I thought now would be the best time to get it underway," Mendenhall said.

"Oh, what project is that?"

You have an old road that runs northwest out of town. We'd like to see it graded and widened and graveled."

Del appeared relieved and smiled as though Mendenhall had gotten bad information. "That 'old back road' has never been more than a trail. Only a few farmers use it anyway, so it doesn't need improving."

Mendenhall leaned forward in his chair. "Did I sound like I was making a request?"

Del's smile faded. Caught flat-footed he had

nothing to say. His expression fell like a puppy who'd been caught having peed on the floor.

"You've got a contractor working on those residential streets. Send them out to start grading and widening that road."

Del finally found his voice. "I think the entire council should agree on something like that." He was ready to pass the buck so fast he'd have submitted his resignation right then and there if asked. "Go see Warren at the auto dealership. If he's okay with it, we'll get right on it."

"I'll go see him, but you need to get that contractor out there to price the job for the entire length of the road. Once you get a good road in that direction, I would imagine a lot more people would use it."

The first thing Mendenhall saw as he approached the auto dealership was a brand new maroon Ram crew cab pick-up leaving the lot with a smiling face behind the wheel. A crowd was looking at new vehicles up and down the aisles. A good many people were getting themselves an early Christmas present, Mendenhall thought, and all on the same day.

Warren was closing a deal when Mendenhall asked for him at the receptionist desk. Mendenhall found a chair in the lobby and prepared to wait. A bustle of people came in and out of the showroom. Basic reasoning would suggest that a dealership in a town like Elmwater would be lucky to sell four or five new vehicles a month. And yet today, potential buyers were lined up at the door. Had Warren found a new line of funds to finance the increase in business?

Warren exited his office with a big smile on his face in the company of a young couple. He repeatedly patted the man on the back and escorted the two to another office. When he saw Mendenhall, the light dimmed behind his eyes. He asked a few questions of his receptionist and led Mendenhall to his office.

"Beautiful day, don't you think?" Warren asked Mendenhall rhetorically. In his mid-sixties, in both temperament and demeanor, Warren was the exact opposite of Del Lupton. At city hall, Warren was willing to play the cooperative colleague. But at the dealership, he was in his comfort zone and king of his realm. He had a toothpick that he never chewed, but let dance with his words in the corner of his mouth. It was a prop, and he could mesmerize people with it as he spoke.

Mendenhall ignored Warren's comment. "I've got a project I'd like you to get started that wasn't on your priority list. "It's grading, widening, and graveling that road that leads out northwest of town."

Warren sat back in his swivel chair and opened a file cabinet beside his desk. He spoke with his head turned away. "We didn't include that project on the list because there's no need to improve that road."

"I talked to the mayor, and he said the same thing. After surveying your town, however, we feel that it's a worthwhile project, and you already have paving contractors working in town."

Warren continued to act preoccupied. "We can only do one thing at a time, you know. Maybe we can address that road later."

"Address it now," Mendenhall emphasized his words. The guy wasn't deaf. He was giving him the stall routine. "Hire another contractor if you need to."

"Well, the money you've given us to work with will be used up real soon."

"Let me assure you there's money earmarked for the city's account. There's no reason why you can't start another project, especially when it wouldn't interfere with anything already going on."

Warren looked at Mendenhall and let the toothpick dance. "If you want us to undertake more projects, we'll need more money in the city account." With that, Warren let the silence settle in the room.

Mendenhall's ears burned, but he didn't flinch. This guy's pretty bold, Mendenhall thought. All the easy money floating around has got this guy thinking his balls are steel. It wasn't a stretch to think Warren and the banker were running a scam with the city's money to sell more vehicles and share in some hefty profits. But if money would keep him distracted, then more money he shall have. Easy money had Warren blinded. Greed would be his downfall.

Warren was playing a dangerous game. Mendenhall thought of the men he'd shot in the face from no further away than he sat from Warren, the people whose throats he'd slit in their sleep, the bombs he'd buried on street corners. Warrens' mouthy comments reminded him to be more watchful and attentive. Warren may have turned the tables for the moment, but he would lose dearly in the end.

"You can rest assured we are here to benefit Elmwater. Another significant deposit will be delivered to the bank today," Mendenhall said.

CHAPTER NINETEEN

ANDY TOOK MISSY TO DINNER but made no mention of the run-in with Whitmire. They made small talk over chicken fried steaks and mashed potatoes – the diner's special of the day.

"So, how do you like working at the bank?" he asked.

"I love it. Ethel's a sweetheart. Like a helpful grandmother. Bonnie and I have a lot in common. She went to Wichita State, too, and she married a fellow from here, Joe Emerson."

"Yes, I know Joe."

"The customers are all so nice. I miss the children, but for now . . ." She stopped mid-sentence as her voice faltered.

"Don't worry about it, Sweetie. Keep focused on

the future. You were saying you liked the bank."

"She turned to him and smiled. "Yes, yes, the bank is nice."

As they left the diner, Andy said, "I want to show you something before I take you home." They got into his truck and headed to the farm. "It's nothing new, Sweetie, just something I fixed up. I hope you like it."

"Of course, I'll like it. Now I'm all excited."

When they reached the farm, Andy took her hand and walked her up the steps and across the porch to a two-person swing with a canvass canopy. He stood beside it and admired the old thing. "It was a mess. I should have had it covered. Birds have been roosting on it for years, and Tipper slept on it whenever I left him outside. I've been cleaning on it for days. I oiled the hinges, and got new seat cushions at the auto parts store." Andy laughed. "But it works now. I hope you like it."

Missy sat on one side of the swing. Andy hustled around to the other side. The view was straight south toward town. The falling rays of an autumn sunset cast a golden glow over Elmwater. Andy and Missy rocked in the swing and enjoyed the peaceful evening.

"It's delightful, Andy. It's perfect."

"Yeah well, Mom and Dad sat here many an evening. I couldn't bring myself to throw it away. I'm glad you like it."

"I like your farm, Andy," she said.

"I'm happy to hear that."

"I like Elmwater, too. It's such a quaint little town, and I mean that in a good way. I suppose some people wouldn't care for such a small place, but I find it a comfort." A minute later, she said. "I'm getting chilly. Do you have a blanket?"

"Be right back." Andy returned with a thick quilt and turned on the porch light. They huddled together under the blanket, her head on his shoulder until darkness overtook the landscape.

"Better get you home, Sweetie."

With the amber porch light reflecting in her eyes, she lifted her head. "Hold me, Andy."

He placed his hand around her shoulders and pulled her closer. He nuzzled cheek to cheek and pulled her legs up onto his lap.

She leaned her head back and gazed into his eyes again. "You're such a gentleman." She smiled. "I won't break like a china vase if you hold me tight." She reached her arm around his neck and kissed his cheek and whispered in his ear. "I don't want to go home tonight, Andy."

He kissed her and lifted her, quilt and all, and carried her into the house.

~ ~ ~ ~

THE NEXT MORNING after he took Missy home, Andy stopped by the diner for breakfast and went back to the farm. He replayed the run-in with Whitmire in his mind. He regretted getting in Whitmire's face over a loan. Now he'd lost someone who might have been on his side over the long haul. Andy had known Whitmire for as long as he could remember. Andy seriously doubted if he'd get the loan now. He'd dug another hole, with no one to blame but himself. He hoped Missy wouldn't hear about it. She would forgive him if she did, but it would upset her, too.

Instead of going back to town, he got on his four-wheeler and headed north across the open prairie onto the abandoned military land. Tipper jumped on the back, and they headed across an expanse of prairie grass and distant vistas. It was a frequent ride whenever Andy wanted to be alone with his thoughts. It was pheasant season, and the birds were moving. They took flight with a rustle of strong wings as the four-wheeler approached. A few jackrabbits darted through the brush. Andy was deep in thought about his miserable situation when he saw something ahead.

He came across a forty foot padlocked cargo container beside a backhoe/front-end loader. Tipper jumped from the four-wheeler and sniffed around. There was no key in the tractor, but it appeared operable. He looked further north and east. There was nothing but prairie grass and a glimpse of Nate Davis's farmhouse roof miles away. The presence of the container and the backhoe was odd, out on this land, miles from anything else. Tipper began barking.

Andy walked to where the dog was scratching in the grass, head down, barking incessantly. And then he saw it, an open hole. As he looked around, footprints were visible, and they were fresh. He got on his hands and knees and peered over the side.

The morning sun was high in the east and illuminated the wall sixty or seventy feet down. The depth of the hole vanished into a tunnel of black. Its diameter was immense. Andy pulled Tipper back and stroked his neck to calm him. In its excitement, the dog could easily misstep and fall into the hole. He walked around it, saw the other footprints, and crushed grass. Andy followed drag marks and saw the enormous steel cover. He couldn't fathom what he saw or any reason for it. But whoever had been here didn't go to the trouble of removing that huge cover just to have something to do.

He had run across an odd situation. Many things had struck him as strange of late. But he'd been looking for something out of the ordinary. Andy shook his head and smiled to himself. Running across this open hole may provide answers, but it raised a dozen more. "Let's go," he yelled to Tipper, and the dog jumped on the back of the four-wheeler. He would go to town because he had questions. And if he could find him, he knew the first person he wanted to ask.

Andy stopped at his house for his pickup and drove to the fairgrounds with Tipper in tow. The barn's concrete floor had been poured. Workmen were welding vertical beams onto base plates for the walls. Corrals were being built and the area for the arena had been graded. He drove by the hospital and the Co-Op. It crossed his mind to check at the bank, but no luck.

Andy was ready to head to the diner for lunch when he saw a familiar vehicle at the Dairy Queen. A faded red welding truck.

The lunch customers, hungry for hamburgers and chicken fingers, were fed and gone. An elderly couple leisurely licked soft serve cones by the window. Romme was by himself on the other side of the room, absorbed with a strawberry sundae.

Andy ordered a soda and walked down the idle. "Well," he said, "we meet again."

Romme glanced up; an irritated expression appeared on his face as though eating a sundae was a religious experience not to be interrupted. When he saw it was Andy, he dropped his gaze. "Oh, hi."

"Mind if I join ya?" Andy sat without waiting for an answer. "You know, I farm most the time, but this is my offseason. I've been looking for extra work for weeks now, but no luck."

"Sorry, pal. I can't help you there."

"Oh, I didn't mean you specifically. I thought maybe you knew someplace in town that was hiring?"

Romme shook his head.

"Maybe I could talk to your boss?" Andy said.

That comment brought Romme out of his passive acquiescence. He licked his spoon and looked directly at Andy. "Look, pal. I appreciate what you did for me the other day, but I don't know anything about jobs around here. You're talking to the wrong person."

"Okay, just thought I'd check. How's your project going?"

"I can't get into that," he said. "I need to be going."

"Before you do, I got something I bet you'd be interested in." Andy wasn't starring, but he remained observant. Now was the time to sprinkle a few bits of information and see if they got a reaction.

"Drove north of my place this morning and I came across this huge hole in the ground."

Romme's face turned white. He had to clear his throat. "What was it, an old well?"

"Oh no, it was much too big for that."

"That's government land, isn't it? Why would you go out there?"

"That's where I shoot birds. You saw that mounted pheasant in my house. Being doing it for years. No one ever tried to stop me, 'cause no one ever goes out there – until now it seems."

"Yeah, your place borders that land, doesn't it?" Romme's question was rhetorical.

"Well, I do know a little about what's going on out there," Romme said. "If you're interested, come with me, and I'll fill you in."

They went to Romme's welding truck. "Hop in. What I have to tell you is private." Romme opened his door and pulled his 9mm pistol from under the seat and stuck it in his left pocket as Andy walked to the other side of the truck. He pointed the truck south out of town and caught the state highway 24 headed west. "I'm not the boss, as you put it, but I am the foreman for a team that's to build and test a new communications tower for the military. It's strictly top secret. If you divulge anything I tell you, I'll inform the general. His M.P.'s will arrest you."

"Does this have anything to do with the projects going on in town?" Andy asked.

"Not that I know of. Our work is for the military."

"So that's why you got stuck on the back road? You had been out to that site?"

"That's why I got stuck," Romme admitted. "That road sure is in bad shape. We were hoping we could use it as a way in and out because we don't want to haul specialized communication equipment through town. "

"Why not?"

"Until the tower is built and tested, it's top secret."

Andy listened carefully to what he was hearing, then thought for a moment. "Listen, I know how you can get into that site without dealing with that back trail. Further east and north is a farmer I know. I bet he'd let you through his land, no problem. It's flat and as wide as you'd ever need."

"That would be great. Can you talk to him soon?"

"I'll talk to him now. Turn this truck around, and I'll show you where he lives."

The men drove back the way they came, past the exit into town, to the next county road ten miles east. They turned north and drove another ten miles to Nate Davis' farm. Andy wasn't in the house more than a few minutes and received Nate's permission.

"Let me show you the gate. We can drive to the site. We can make sure the way is clear," Andy said.

"Did your friend ask any questions?"

"No, he's too busy for that. I asked if I could drive through his land, and he said okay."

Two miles down the county road, they came to an open gate. They traveled across a winding, but level path, past discarded farm equipment rusting in the sun, and over a broken down fence that marked the government property. A few miles further south and four miles west and the yellow backhoe was visible next to the container.

"The distance is farther than coming down that old road but a whole lot smoother," Andy said.

"Much better," Romme replied. "Listen, you know about this now, and you said you needed a job, right?"

"Right."

"The other men will be back tomorrow, and we begin work on the base of the tower. Be out here at seven, and I'll see if I can put you on."

"I'll be here."

"And remember, top secret."

CHAPTER TWENTY

THE NEXT DAY six men arrived in three trucks and stopped at the motel on the highway. Romme got in with them and directed them to the open missile silo by the new route. They made it to the site as dawn was breaking. The trucks carried more steel I-beams and angle iron, ropes, harnesses, lights, hydraulic lifts for raising and lowering material into the silo, new welding hoses, and acetylene tanks. Andy showed up on his 4-wheeler and began unloading trucks.

Andy closely watched the activity around him. Before he went to bed, he replayed his conversation with Romme at the Dairy Queen. The notion that this tower project had nothing to do with the construction activities in town didn't ring true. When Romme said everything was top secret and not to breathe a word of it, he knew he was on to something.

Let his neighbors bask in illusions of lady luck. He knew better. He was disgusted with all of them now. They had all turned their backs on him, chastising, critical, condescending. At a time when he most needed a helping hand, all he received was patronizing lectures as though he were too dense to benefit from their words of wisdom. All of them – since the death of the Taylor Carson, Andy couldn't think of a single person talking to him like an adult. And when he made a simple suggestion, they investigate the source of the 'free government money' he became a pariah.

For now, he would work, watch, and wait.

THE ROCKET WOULD BE APPROXIMATELY SEVENTY FEET LONG, plus or minus, depending on the final thrust impulse calculation necessary to get the warhead to the target. The length of the engine would be adjusted to provide the correct amount of fuel burn to get the rocket to the apex of its trajectory. The specific length of the engine would be determined once the total weight of the payload bomb, nose cone, guidance controls, and exhaust nozzle was calculated.

The blast floor had to be built low enough to keep the entire rocket construction hidden below ground. The blast pad would be built ninety feet below the rim of the silo. The men erected two hydraulic lifts on either side of the hole and stretched steel cables between them to provide stability. The cables would also be used to lower men and materials.

The men took advantage of the existing girders in the walls to build the blast floor. They lowered two men one hundred feet in harnesses. When they were in place, an I-beam was lowered on hydraulic cables. The beam would span the silo from wall to wall. The men welded the beam in place ninety feet below the surface.

Shorter lengths of I-beam were cut and welded to the center span, and then to the girder directly across from it in the wall. Andy worked with a torch cutting the shorter pieces of steel I-beam to correct lengths. Building the steel web to support the blast floor took a week.

When the work was well underway, Romme brought Mendenhall with him to the site after Mendenhall returned from a trip to Kansas City. Romme was anxious to talk to him and to show Mendenhall how the work at the site was progressing.

"Are they going to get that back road graded?" Romme asked. "We have another way into the site, but we still have a lot of heavy items to bring in – the rocket sections mainly. We still need that road," Romme said as he headed straight north out of Elmwater.

Mendenhall stared out the window and scowled. "I have enough on my mind. I can't say for sure when they will work on the road. I made an additional deposit into the city's account."

"Here's that back road," Romme said as he turned left on the fork that led northwest out of town. The ride was smooth in stretches, but erosion trenches, almost impossible to see before they were hit, popped up left and right. The road oscillated in places; high side left to high side right, enough to make it necessary to grab onto something within the truck. A few miles up the road, Romme turned due east across the shallow ditch beside the dead tree. "The site is straight ahead."

"As soon as you're ready, Hanania will bring up the sections of the rocket," Mendenhall said.

"The way things are going, we'll be ready long before that road gets fixed," Romme said. "The only other way in is almost in front of a guy's farmhouse. We'll have to move them in the middle of the night."

"Don't worry, they'll be wrapped and strapped down on a trailer," Mendenhall said. "No one is going to see any rocket sections."

"Okay, okay," Romme said. "We'll be ready in a week."

At the site, the men were lowering 2 x 2-foot pieces of 1/2-inch 6061-T6 aluminum alloy plate and welding them on the beams. When finished, they'd have a 400 square foot blast floor. Mendenhall stayed in the truck and watched. Three men worked around the silo, unloading alloy plate, connecting it to a clamp on a pulley system, and lowering them, one by one, into the hole.

Mendenhall didn't watch long before the size of the hole intrigued him. He wanted to see the scope and progress of the work. He got on his hands and knees and peered into the depths. A string of lights on two walls illuminated the cavernous hole. He could see men welding on the platform. Two men pulled another plate from a panel truck and sat it on the ground edge up. Another man pulled slack in the cable and the clamp over to the plate. Once fastened, the pulley system moved back over the hole, and the plate lowered.

Mendenhall looked closely at the men. Three were Hispanic. He didn't know them, he didn't talk to them, but he had seen them before. Three of the men he knew. They were Arabs, and he had worked with them before. Another man, the one who lowered the metal plate was white. He was wearing denim overalls and a baseball cap. He looked like every other farmer Mendenhall had seen in town. Mendenhall studied his face and took note of his features. Who was he, and why was he here?

Mendenhall looked around. Romme was rummaging about in one of the trucks. The thought that Romme had put a local to work had Mendenhall seething. He had enough concerns without the genuine possibility that someone outside the entrusted group might learn the truth and alert authorities. If Romme didn't have the right answers, Mendenhall would slit the farmer's throat when the other workers were elsewhere, tie an I-beam to his leg, and drop him into this bottomless pit. But before he could talk to Romme, a gasp came from the men standing at the silo edge, followed by an echoing scream that rose from the depths. A piece of metal had slipped from the clamp and fallen on a welder. It hit him in the right thigh as he sat in his harness and tore a gash in his leg. He was pulled to the surface immediately. Blood saturated his pants.

The man moaned. His arms and legs were dangling. Hs head rolled back and forth. Other men cut him from his harness. They pulled him out of his pants to better see the wound. Andy took off his shirt and wrapped a tourniquet high on his thigh. A chunk of flesh fell open like a flap. Andy pressed it back into place, put a clean glove over the injury, and bandaged it as best he could with strips of fabric torn from the man's pants.

"He has to get to the hospital fast," Andy said. "I can take him."

Romme was right there in the midst of the effort. He helped pull him away from the silo edge and cut the man's pants into strips. He movements were automatic, the same as assisting an injured comrade on the battlefield. "No, I'll take him. I know where the hospital is."

The men placed him across the back seat of a van. "Take a break. We'll be back when we can." He motioned to Mendenhall. The sliding side door slammed shut, and the van sped west.

Mendenhall turned and looked at the injured man in the back seat. He was indifferent to the entire event. He also knew they couldn't take the man to the hospital. Romme barreled across the prairie at fifty miles an hour.

"Slow down?"

"Just as soon as I get out of sight of the other men."

"Who in the hell is that farmer?"

"Don't worry about him," Romme said. "He just wanted a job."

"Are you out of your mind? He knows where

you're working. He knows what you're doing. We'll have to get rid of him."

"He thinks we're building a communication tower. I told him everything was top secret. He's not going to tell anyone." Romme slowed the vehicle and glanced at Mendenhall. "You're worried about nothing. It's the opposite. He'll help me keep tabs on the rest of the town folk. If anything new happens in town, he'll tell me about it."

Two hours later, Romme returned, but without Mendenhall. Romme chose to call it a day. Romme and his men headed to the motel by the route past the Davis farm. Andy headed to the hospital.

ANDY DROVE HIS FOUR-WHEELER to the house. He left a cloud of dust behind his truck speeding into town and took the winding hospital steps two at a time. Out of breath, Andy approached the nurse's station.

"Guy brought in several hours ago. Big gash on his leg. What room is he in?"

The nurse checked the intake records. "Nobody's come in this afternoon," she said. "

"What time is it?" Andy asked. He looked at the clock on the wall behind her. "It doesn't matter the time, it was after lunch, four hours ago, I'd say."

"I don't have any . . . "

"Could he still be in emergency?"

"I'd know about that, too. No one's down there."

"Check again."

"I've been here all afternoon. No new admittances."

"What if he was sent on over to Bridgedale?"

"I'd still have a record of it if he came here first."

"Are you sure? Check again."

The nurse said nothing but shook her head slowly.

Andy placed both hands on the counter and stared at the nurse. "He was hurt bad – real bad." Bewildered, Andy finally turned and walked toward the front door.

CHAPTER TWENTY-ONE

THE WAREHOUSE COMPLEX in North Kansas City was virtually abandoned. The driveways and parking areas were a spider web of cracks. In places, slabs of broken concrete fell on top of one another. The docks were narrow, the roofs leaked. A fence company with storage at the other end of the drive, whose men came by once a week to pick up supplies, was the only tenant ever seen about the place.

Once the rice bales were inside, the overhead door was locked, and the windows draped with black plexiglass curtains. Access to the warehouse came through a side door of unused office space. A continually running exhaust fan pulled interior air to the outside. Asim's men opened the two rice bales and placed the lead cases on separate workbenches.

In full protective gear, the men opened the first one. The inner glass case was warm to the touch. The Geiger counter on the workbench clicked at a slow pace. Asim opened the glass lid. The radioactive sensor clicked more rapidly, but well within tolerable limits.

They removed the uranium from the glass enclosure. The piece was flat, twenty-two by twenty-two inches and two and a half inches thick. Each piece weighed twenty-five kilos (55 pounds). At a drill press with a fixed die, the man began the process of pressing the metal into the shape, much like half a cantaloupe with the fruit scooped out. They would work on the other uranium slabs the same way.

Asim was busy building other components for two bombs. He was especially pleased with the barometric pressure detonation device of his invention. The ideal detonation altitude was 1000 feet above the ground. The target lay at 400 feet above sea level, one thousand feet lower than their current location. His device would require no computer instructions or complicated inputs as the warhead descended. It was a simple altimeter design attached to a bubble switch.

Right before launch, he would get a barometric pressure reading from the airport at the target location and set that reading into the warhead altimeter. When the warhead descended to 1400 feet above sea level, the desired altitude above the city, the increasing air pressure would snap the switch contacts together. The electric circuit would close. The six bands of TNT around the uranium shell would implode instantaneously and symmetrically. The radioactive chain reaction would occur in less than a blink of an eye. The resulting heat and blast wave of a 20 kiloton atom bomb would incinerate everything below it in a four-mile radius with extensive damage to every structure ten miles out in all directions.

A nuclear bomb required assembly with the precision of a fine timepiece. Asim knew the intricacies of atomic fission and the requirements of creating an atomic chain reaction. The greater the heat and energy shock wave produced, the better. But the attack would succeed if the bomb got close to the intended target with at least half of the fissionable material chain reacting before the remaining material blew apart. Their dirty bomb would create radioactive fallout that would kill thousands. It would be years before the land mass over which it exploded could be used again for human habitation. The target was Washington D.C. Asim knew his bomb would effectively destroy the capital of the United States regardless of how many buildings fell.

The two halves of uranium, shaped like two halves of a volleyball and approximately the same size, would be secured to a three-inch thick oak board. A symmetrical web of six high explosive TNT charges would encircle the uranium ball. All charges would be wired and set to explode simultaneously, producing an instantaneous implosion. After wiring, a tamper made of titanium steel would encase the bomb to facilitate a maximum inward implosion. A high voltage battery secured to the platform and the barometric bubble switch would complete the device.

Asim was patient yet excited. As the men worked on pressing the uranium slabs into shape, he worked on the TNT harness. He was an expert at such work. The placement and detonation of the explosives would crush the uranium into itself. A billion escaping neutrons from the uranium mass would crash into one another. Each crash of neutrons would create an exponential increase in the number of escaping neutrons crashing into more escaping neutrons. A blinding wave of light, heat, and energy would result. And it would all happen in less than a millisecond.

Once the men had shaped the first two uranium slabs, the delicate assembly commenced. The slabs for the second bomb were machined and assembled like the first. When complete, the bombs rested in lead-lined crates inside cargo tool boxes wrapped in canvass. They were ready to be delivered to Elmwater, Kansas.

CHAPTER TWENTY-TWO

MENDENHALL BROODED in his motel room. The flippant and dismissive remarks of councilman Warren had him on edge. Mendenhall had plunked down an additional ten million dollars for a total of twenty million. The townspeople had visions of erecting a new building dedicated to a library, and traffic lights at four intersections. There wasn't an intersection in town that saw as many as thirty cars an hour, and yet, having functioning traffic lights seemed to be a prestige thing for the town.

Warren must have surmised there was a lot more money to be had. Rather than acquiesce to Mendenhall's simple request to grade a road, Warren was playing hardball and insisting more money was needed to proceed with projects already on the drawing board. Whatever his game, Mendenhall intended to cut it short. He was proficient at terminating people face to face, but he could make accidents happen, too.

Another matter bothered him even more. Romme violated one of the most important rules of the plan. No one outside the group was to know what was going on. Outside eyes and loose lips could ruin everything, waste millions of dollars, and if that happened, Mendenhall knew he would only have days to live. He would be hunted relentlessly until his head was on a platter.

Romme had brought in an outsider to the project. When Romme returned to the motel, Mendenhall was watching through his window. He opened his door and summoned Romme. "Anyone ask about our injured man?" Mendenhall asked.

"No. The other men may want to hear some answers later, but they don't ask questions."

"Tell me again why you put that local farmer to work. Don't you realize the jeopardy that puts us in?"

"I had to. He found the open hole."

"What?" The information caught Mendenhall by surprise.

"Yeah, he lives in the last farmhouse out of town the way we went this morning. He was out driving around on a 4-wheel bike and ran across it. He came to me asking questions. He wondered if I knew anything about it. I had to feed him a story. I had to get him on my side or who knows who might have started looking around."

"Okay, okay, then. You did the right thing, I suppose." Mendenhall sat on the edge of the bed. "But we have to make sure he doesn't make it out of town."

"Ain't nobody going to be leaving. We both know that." Romme said.

"Shut up. You're not listening. He's seen us, you for certain. He knows your truck. Before the launch, he'll know a lot more. He's got to be dealt with personally. If he slips away for one reason or another, he can fill in authorities. They'll be able to track us."

"Whatever you say. When we're ready, I'll take care of him," Romme said.

Mendenhall paced the room for a minute. "I want to go out to his place, see what he drives, talk to him. See what he has to say."

"I thought you wanted to keep clear of him."

"Well, you ruined that idea, now didn't you?"

"Listen, he drives a beat-up white pickup with blue trim."

Mendenhall had already decided. "Let's go out there. As you said, he may be a pipeline to what's on the minds of the other folks in town."

They got into Romme's truck. As they headed north on Main, Romme said, "what if he asks about our injured man?"

"Like we said before. Tell him the guy's at the hospital."

Romme shook his head. "Bad idea. Too easy to check."

"Hell, he doesn't care. He's not going to ask about that?"

"Just saying," Romme replied. "We should have a story in case he does."

"Let me worry about that."

There was no pickup in the drive when they arrived at the house. They got out, walked around the shed, and sat on the porch. They were about to leave when a cloud of dust signaled the approach of a vehicle. Andy drove up. Missy was with him. Andy helped her from the truck, and they walked to the house hand in hand. Mendenhall took note of the truck and memorized the license plate number.

"Something else happen?" Andy asked.

"No," Romme replied, "our project manager wanted to meet you in person. This is Mr. Mendenhall."

"Hello, Andy Branson."

"Glad to meet you." Mendenhall extended his hand then turned to Missy. "And you too, Mrs. Branson." He thought she looked familiar.

"No," she said. "we're not married."

"Do you want to come inside?" Andy asked.

"Just for a few minutes."

Inside, they sat around the cluttered kitchen table. Missy got the men bottles of water from the fridge.

"So," Mendenhall began, "the project's construction is strictly for military purposes. It has nothing to do with the public. That's why it's a top secret project. I understand you ran across it while motoring around. That's fine as long as you keep it to your self."

"I intend to."

Mendenhall didn't like the idea of discussing the

project in front of the woman, but she probably already knew something about it. She might be useful in keeping track of this guy's whereabouts.

"I see a lot of activity going on in town. Any big news?" Mendenhall asked.

"No, not really," Andy said. "Everyone is happy from what I've heard, but nobody tells me much. I'm the black sheep of the community right now."

"Oh, why's that?"

"It's a long story, but it'll blow over," Andy said. "Probably when all the money's gone. So how long's it going to take to finish the tower?"

"As long as it takes," Mendenhall said. "We're under no time restrictions."

"How tall is it going to be?"

"One hundred and fifty feet above the ground. " Mendenhall tried to smile. "You sure ask a lot of questions."

"Just curious. So what happened to the injured guy?"

Romme glanced at Mendenhall.

Mendenhall cleared his throat. "Bad news, I'm sorry to say. He passed out on us, then died. He went into shock, I think, or he bled to death."

"Died! He couldn't have bled to death. I put a tourniquet on him. I saw the wound. It took a chunk of flesh out of his leg, but it didn't cut an artery. He wasn't bleeding that bad."

"I can't answer all that. When we got to the hospital, he was dead."

"Where did you take him?"

"That town a few miles north."

"To a hospital? You know we have a local one.

You said you were taking him there." Andy grabbed his head with both hands incredulous over what he was hearing. "No wonder he died."

"No, to a funeral home. He was already dead, so we didn't go into the hospital."

"Why there? We have a funeral home in town. Don't you have to tell the police about something like that?"

Mendenhall tried to act concerned and sympathetic. "He was military, a specialist in the Air Force. They'll handle it from here on." Mendenhall smiled inside as he watched Andy crumble emotionally with confusion and disbelief. "I don't like it any more than you do. I know you did your best to help him."

Mendenhall stood to leave. Romme put his hand on Andy's shoulder. "I'm sorry, too. I know you did your best, but now you know. It was an accident. His family will be well taken care of. See you in the morning." The two men left the house.

Once in Romme's truck, Mendenhall spoke up. "Give me his phone number and find out where the woman stays."

~ ~ ~ ~

Missy PULLED UP A KITCHEN CHAIR and sat beside Andy. She put her hand on his neck and rubbed her thumb against his cheek. The closed front door held his gaze, then he turned and looked into her eyes.

"You know, I don't know those two men at all. They're lying," he said. "That worker spoke nothing but Spanish on the job if he spoke at all. If he was U.S. military, why didn't I ever hear him speak English? Not once. They got rid of him because that project is top secret all right, but not for the reason they say."

"Should you report it?" she asked.

"Probably, but to who? Police Chief Stevens is benefiting as much as anyone with this free money campaign. I know they are tied together, this communication tower and what's going on in town. No, I think I'll keep going to work and keep an eye out. "

"For one thing, I know we're not building a tower out there. We're installing a support structure half way down a humongous hole. It would take a thousand truckloads of concrete even to come close to filling that old missile hole to provide proper support for a tower. Why would anyone do that when you could drill a new hole a tenth the size and have your underground support ready to go?"

"Andy, please be careful."

He turned and hugged her and kissed her cheek. "I'll be careful, baby. And you keep your eyes open too, especially around the bank. Let me know of anything suspicious or irregular.

"Well, I've seen that older guy before," she said.

"The one called Mendenhall?"

She nodded.

"Where?"

"At the bank. He's been in several times. Never transacts any business. Always asks to see Mr. Whitmire."

Andy got up and paced the kitchen. "See," he

said, "another odd activity. Think about it. Why would a guy who says he's in charge of a top secret military project need to see a small town banker?" It certainly wouldn't be to borrow money. You follow me?"

"Yes, I get what you're talking about, Andy. All the more, I think you should report it," her voice urgent, her eyes imploring.

He knelt at her feet, an easy smile on his face. "Sweetie, do you think I'd ever do something dangerous that would keep me away from you? I need a little more time; that's all." He brought her closer. "I'll find out what's going on; then I'll take all the information to the authorities."

CHAPTER TWENTY-THREE

O N HANANIA'S FARM in Wichita, he and Raghib rented a forty-foot open trailer with high side rails and loaded the five remaining 15-foot long rocket engine sections with the help of a hydraulic crane. Each 15-foot section weighed 12,000 lbs. Based on the information given to him by Asim, Hanania calculated he needed 72 feet of fuel for the necessary two minutes of engine burn, so the fifth section was cut to 12 feet in length before loading. They wrapped the engine sections in a heavy tarp, tied them down, then covered the load with another tarp. When the trailer was ready to roll, it looked like any other cargo trailer one might see traveling down the road. The men left Wichita after dark and arrived in Elmwater at 1:00 a.m.

They pulled into the motel parking lot where Romme waited.

For the next month, the workmen assembled the rocket sections. Andy kept his mouth shut and worked every day. Christmas came and went without anyone at the site paying a passing comment to the holiday. Missy cooked Andy a feast Christmas evening with roasted turkey and all the fixings, and they exchanged gifts. Andy bought a silver necklace. Missy bought him a fur-lined cap with ear flaps. He chuckled agreeably when he opened the present as though she was kidding him, but once he tried it on, Andy never left the house without it when he went to work.

The assembly work began fifteen feet above the blast floor. Four support I- beams were welded horizontally into the silo walls. These four beams would rest under, and support the rocket. The exhaust nozzle was seven feet long with an 18-inch wide throat and a 42-inch wide exhaust bell. At launch, the exhaust bell was narrow enough to pass by the steel beams that supported the rocket.

The DeLaval type nozzle had a flat face for connecting to the base of the rocket. The exhaust nozzle was attached as the rocket section lay on the ground. The detonators were inserted deep into the solid fuel at the base of the rocket. A round ceramic seal set into place and bolts secured the nozzle onto the missile. Then, the fifteen-foot rocket section with the exhaust nozzle in place was lowered and set on the steel supports.

Andy was aghast when he first laid eyes on the rocket fins and the exhaust nozzle. His jaw dropped.

Andy couldn't believe what he saw. He dared not look directly at anyone. The sight was incomprehensible. For a time, his brain became so jumbled with thoughts, he could hardly remember his name.

From then on, Andy looked for ways to damage the rocket. But he was restricted to working above ground, cutting steel and angle iron, attaching rocket sections to the lift, and helping the other men in and out of harnesses. Someone was always watching. He could try to drop a rocket section into the hole by letting it slip off the crane, but that would get someone killed. The other men did all of the precision work of wiring and joining the sections together.

Andy knew the sections contained solid rocket fuel. He thought about driving a rod through the side of a section in hopes it might cause a lateral burn through at launch. But the heavy pipe and sheet metal skin would require a hammer to drive something through the rocket wall, and he was watched too closely for that.

Late in the day the exhaust nozzle was attached and lowered into the hole, Romme approached Andy and pulled him aside. "I know you realize we're not building a tower here, and I want to explain," Romme said. "When I said everything was top secret, I meant it. The less everyone knows, including those at the work site, the better. At least the higher up's think so."

"This projectile will test a new solid fuel formula. The launch exhaust will ruin the silo. That's why we're building it here, in an old hole."

"When's it going to be fired?" Andy asked.

"I don't know."

"Where's it going to land?"

"What with all the questions?" Romme said. "I work here like you do. I would imagine the Gulf of Mexico, but I don't know. Nobody's told me about such things, and I've learned it's better not to ask. You've done good work, and I just wanted to be upfront with you. When they fire the thing, they'll be plenty of people here to watch. You can come too if you want. It won't be a secret by then. Tracking satellites will collect all the data the military wants."

Andy nodded." Okay, thanks for the update. I was a little confused." Romme turned, and Andy watched him walk away. Andy's gaze bore into the man's back. I must look the part of clueless sodbuster, he thought. Andy didn't believe a word of what Romme said.

He'd heard enough blatant lies from Romme and his partner that he wasn't inclined to believe another word from either of them. The fact that he was lied to at the beginning about a tower was evidence enough for Andy that the real purpose of the machine hadn't been divulged, and wouldn't be. He had to find out for himself and stop it. The machine in the hole wasn't ready yet. He still had time.

Two moveable vanes, fifteen inches wide and extending ten inches from the base of the exhaust cone were attached to maneuver the rocket toward the proper heading once the rocket was a mile above the earth. The vanes were connected to motors in the nose cone by a titanium alloy cable.

The guidance coordinates would be set right before the launch to the exact trajectory azimuth. The cables would run up either side of the rocket, one to ignite the engine, the other to the controls that would set the direction of flight.

As the rocket assembly ascended, 3/4 inch metal tubes, one for the flight controls and the other for the ignition cables, were attached on the exterior of the rocket frame. The tubes were cemented to the metal skin and fastened with U-brackets every two feet. The wires in each tube were pulled upward as the rocket assembly climbed to the surface. The work was slow but steady. The rocket grew, reaching higher and higher, rising from the depths of the silo.

Then, at the end of one work day, Romme instructed one of the Arabs to remain behind for the night. He could sit in the cab of one of the trucks if the night got too cold. There was a loaded rifle in the truck cab. From then on, a guard was on duty whenever the work crew was away.

CHAPTER TWENTY-FOUR

M ENDENHALL REMEMBERED SEEING the young woman who was at the farmhouse, as well. One afternoon, he waited in the bank parking lot. The previous night's snowfall covered the grassy areas in a blanket of white, but the parking lot was open after a day of traffic, and the roads were clear. Shortly after 3:30, three women bundled in winter coats, left the bank, and walked to their cars.

Mendenhall had no trouble identifying his target. He watched her get in a white Ford Focus and head across town. She stopped at the drugstore. Mendenhall wrote down her tag number. She returned with a small bag and proceeded to a residential area. She pulled into a drive beside a two-story strip of apartments and went into the last one on the right on the ground floor. As Mendenhall sat in his car, he thought to himself. If he wanted to find her, she'd most likely be in one of three places–the bank, that farmhouse up north, or this apartment on Peach Street.

The project was coming off smoothly. There were only a few loose ends to contend with–the curious farm boy with all the questions, and the defiant city councilman who hadn't so much as lifted a shovel to improve that back road even when he had plenty of money to do so. He planned to have them both dealt with individually. His third problem was history. He and Romme strangled the injured Hispanic worker, stripped him of all clothing threw him in a ditch and covered him with branches. If the coyotes and raccoons did their jobs, his body would be nothing but a few scattered bones if ever found.

ROMME WATCHED THE PROGRESS being made assembling the rocket and knew if the warhead were ready, they could complete everything ahead of schedule. From the very beginning, the mission struck him as both brilliantly conceived and next to impossible to achieve. But he was paid to work, so that's what he did. The target was Washington D.C., a small city geographically. The launch date was the day of the president's annual State of the Union Address, January 21st. The chamber would be packed with visitors and invitees in the upper gallery. Justices of the Supreme Court would be there. Cabinet Secretaries, military brass, a majority of the 425 House

Representatives and 100 Senators, and most importantly, the Speaker of the House, the Vice President, and the President of the United States would all be in attendance.

If the bomb exploded over the Capital Building, everyone would vaporize in an explosion of millions of degrees Fahrenheit. A fireball would move at the speed of sound from the center of the explosion with back-pressure winds moving at over five hundred miles per hour. Even if it missed the U.S.capital but hit anywhere along the eastern seaboard politicians would be terrified, unable to respond immediately. Chaos would ensue. The bomb would kill tens of thousands, and the country would plunge into turmoil long enough for Islamic Fighters to make substantial inroads into conquering the land.

Romme readily admitted he knew nothing about rockets or atomic bombs. His expertise was in operating heavy machinery and construction. This whole project couldn't be more than a shot in the dark, a desperate action of blood-thirsty religious zealots. Still, if men like Mendenhall, Hanania, and Asim could get this thing in the air and it exploded anywhere over the United States, they would bask in the glory of their compatriots for the rest of their days. Never mind that they missed their original target.

As he milled about and watched the assembly of the rocket, Romme realized the advantageous position in which he found himself. Never before had he been a part of a mission where money was doled out to keep other people preoccupied. He wanted a bigger cut. He worked hard and knew he was an intricate cog in the operation. He may never again be so close to so much money.

The others in the main team were all Islamic Jihadist. A guaranteed pass to paradise was the only reward they sought. But Romme was to be paid for his work. Once he thought it over, the money promised him seemed a pittance, and the rocket had to launch successfully before he got paid. He had no control over whether the rocket worked or not, and he'd worked too hard to end up with nothing.

His mind was incredulous with the incongruent notion held by his comrades that killing human beings because of the ideas they held resulted in a guaranteed path to eternal life. It made no sense; it held no victory for him. Romme was a Muslim in name, but he was not devout. The older he got, the less he cared for ceremony and prayers. The others could do as they wished. Getting paid was his only concern. He realized with a fleeting sense of sadness that his motivation was as void of humanity as theirs.

Romme formulated a plan to line his pockets. It was his only chance to make a big score. After this was over, he may serve in other conflicts or clandestine adventures, but he would receive only soldiers pay for his keen aim and a willingness to kill. Men like him were not that hard to find. That evening in his motel room, Romme rolled about on his bed, half asleep. At 1:00 a.m. Romme slipped out of the motel with a roll of duct tape, a pair of handcuffs, and a 4" knife that folded into its handle. In the ammo pouch on his thigh was a syringe and a vial of liquid. On the other thigh was strapped a Glock 9mm pistol. He walked in the shadows to Ralph Whitmire's house. The house was a split-level brick home, modest, yet built on a knoll in heavily treed area of town. There were no gates, no obvious indications of outdoor security.

Whitmire and his wife were in their late-fifties. He wasn't sure if anyone else lived in the house but suspected not. He could tell where the master bedroom was by the large translucent glass window of the master bath. He pulled on gloves and a mask and jimmied the window into a spare bedroom. Romme slid through the window with the effort of a snake slithering through the grass. He made his way to the master bedroom and watched. Moonlight filtered through cracked blinds. Two bodies were in bed.

He only wanted Whitmire. Back at the motel, he had thought about what to do with anyone else he came upon. He could sedate them, and they would probably sleep through the night. Now he faced the problem of what to do with this woman in the bed, but he knew all along what he would do. He would take the quick and easy path to rid himself of unwanted distractions. He couldn't chance it that Mrs. Whitmire might wake up early, see her husband gone, and call the police. He filled the syringe with Propofol and stuck it into the woman's arm. She would be dead in her sleep in less than twenty seconds.

Romme stepped to the other side of the bed and rapped Whitmire in the head with a sharp knuckle. Whitmire groaned. Romme hit him again.

Whitmire's eyes popped open and with them came a gasp.

"Get dressed fatso, we've got places to go."

"Who are you?"

Romme didn't say another word. He pulled Whitmore from the bed, locked an arm behind him, and threw him into the wall. "I said, get dressed."

Whitmire blubbered and whined as he pulled on his pants and shoes. "We're going to the bank," Rommes said. "Get the keys. We're taking your car."

It was after 2:00 a.m. The town was locked down tight. The men drove to the back of the building. Romme pushed Whitmire ahead, into the bank, and whispered in his ear. "How much cash in the place?"

"I don't know," Whitmire whimpered, "maybe ten thousand or so."

Romme grabbed his arm and bent it behind his back. Whitmire cried out. "Listen, fat boy. If you don't play ball, I'm going to gut you like the pig you are." Whitmire fell to his knees and yelped in pain.

"It's all in the safe."

"Open it!"

"I can't. It's on a time lock."

Romme hauled off and busted him with a punch in the side of the head. Whitmire keeled over like a drunk sailor. Woozy and bleeding from the forehead, Whitmire sat up.

"I don't believe you," Romme said. "Open it, 'cause if you don't . . ." Romme didn't even bother to finish the sentence.

Any remaining resistance Whitmire may have had drained into an acquiescent puddle of defeat. He opened the vault and pulled back the door.

The vault was a mine of cash slots more than a foot deep. Four slots were full of hundreds. Romme handcuffed Whitmire with his hands behind his back, sat him in the far corner, and filled bags with cash. He left the dollar bills but still had eight bags stuffed when finished.

Romme put the money bags near the back door, then grabbed Whitmire by the handcuffs and pushed him toward the back. Just outside came a strong and steady voice, " Hold it right there, mister. Police."

The voice came from his right, between him and Whitmire. Romme pulled out the knife and put it to the banker's throat. "Don't be too hasty, officer. Mr. Whitmire here would like to live another day." The moonlight was sufficient to see. The cop was pressed against the building ten feet from the door. His squad car was parked across the alley blocking the direction Whitmire's car faced.

"Don't try anything. Give up while you can." The cop pushed the mike button on his shoulder. "Base, are you there?"

There was no time to talk. Romme thrust Whitmire toward the cop. He rolled into the alley and threw the knife. Whitmire sprawled at the cop's feet. The knife hit the officer but didn't stick. A wild shot careened off the asphalt. A second shot from the officer hit the back of the building across the alley. By then, Romme had rolled a second time. He came up and fired a single shot into the cop's face. The man fell dead. Whitmire was on his knees, blubbering in terror. Romme put a bullet in the back of his head.

Romme retrieved his knife and threw the money bags in the back of the car. He backed out of the alley and drove to the motel where he unloaded the bags in the tool bin of his truck. He drove back to Whitmire's house and parked the car in the drive. Then Romme set out to cover the fifteen blocks back to the motel. He kept to overgrown vacant lots, walking between houses, avoiding street lights that poked holes in the darkness. Four shots fired. He could only hope no one heard them. So far, there was no discernible activity on the streets.

Romme had intended to take Whitmire out to the highway and run over him and stage his car to make it look like he'd been hit by another vehicle while changing a tire. If he had been able to do it that way, it was possible the cops would think Mrs. Whitmire had died of a heart attack. Now, all bets were off. The robbery would be discovered, of course, but with a dead cop, the whole town would become wary. Outsiders would come in to investigate. It wasn't good, but he'd made his play. No one had stopped him yet.

He walked into the motel parking lot and slipped into his truck. Quietly Romme rolled out of the lot. He was headed back to Kansas City for a few days. He needed to hide his money.

CHAPTER TWENTY-FIVE

T HE DEAD OFFICER BEHIND the bank was Jason Downs, Andy's closest friend. When Jason didn't respond on his two-way after contacting the police station, a search began. Within the hour Officer Downs was found along with the bloody corpse of Ralph Whitmire. By 3:00 A.M, the alley behind the bank was abuzz with humanity.

The bank's back door was not locked. Once inside, the authorities quickly discovered the ransacked vault. The motive and reason for the deaths of the two men now determined, the bodies were photographed, their clothing examined. Officer Downs' service revolver lay on the ground near him. The bodies were loaded into ambulances and taken to Salina for complete autopsies.

By daybreak, the town was awash in gossip and

hearsay. The bank was closed and would remain so until further notice. Residents living around the bank were all questioned. No one saw or heard a thing. When police tried to contact Mrs. Whitmire about her husband's death, they received no response at the door. They noticed the jimmied side window and broke down the front door. They found her dead in her bed. The entire house and yard were roped off as another crime scene. Even a rookie cop would assume a connection to events at the bank and her body was sent to Salina, too.

Missy arrived for work at the bank at 8:00. She found the bank cordoned off with yellow tape, police vehicles all around the place. Ethel met her in the parking lot.

"Mr. Whitmire's dead," Ethel said. She blew her nose into a wadded tissue.

Missy stopped in her tracks. The news was truly unnerving, but Missy was in better shape to handle the news than Ethel. The older woman had worked for the man for more than a decade. Ethel's eyes were bloodshot. She kept trying to use the same worn out tissue. Missy grabbed a wad of clean ones from her purse. "Here, take these," she said. "Let me drive you. Do you want to go home or where?"

Ethel could only shake her head and blow her nose.

"Well then, come with me for now," Missy said.

Missy drove straight to Andy's house. His truck was gone. Headed back into town, she ran into Andy coming her way.

"I headed over to your place as soon as I heard," Andy said through his open window.

"Guess where we've been?"

"Well turn around. Let's go back to the house. I need to talk to you."

Andy hugged Missy when she got out of the car. "It's bad, awful bad," he said. "Morning, Mrs. Akers. Please come inside."

Tipper bounded around the ladies, taking a special whiff of the older woman. "Down boy. Get down. You stay outside."

"I'm out of fresh coffee." He brought them each a bottle of water without being asked and twisted the cap on a bottle for himself.

Ethel took a seat in the rocker, and Andy sat on the couch with Missy. "They killed Jason." The words caught in his throat."

Where?" Missy asked.

"Behind the bank with Whitmire. He must have caught them in the act."

"Do they know who it was?"

"Not yet. Don't know how many or nothing. But I'll bet you a thousand dollars it's got something to do with all the free money floating around town. Someone knew who Whitmire was and how to get to him."

"You think it was someone local?" Ethel asked. The idea made her pale.

"Anybody been asking a lot of questions lately at the bank?"

Missy shook her head.

"Anything at all suspicious?"

"Nothing Andy. The place has been a zoo for more than a month, but everyone seemed delighted. No one was turned down for a loan that I know of, and nobody would know how much money the bank had in cash."

"Yeah, but the bank would have to have more cash on hand than usual to handle the flow of new checks. Someone around town realized that. Armed robbery and two counts of first-degree murder. I'm going to see to it that someone hangs for it."

"Andy, please. Don't talk like that. Let the police do their job. I don't want you to get hurt."

"Jason was my friend." Andy grabbed his head in his hands and covered his face. His body visibly shrunk in total despair, and he turned away from Missy. He didn't make a sound, but she knew he was crying.

She wrapped her arms around his shoulders and put her cheek against his back. "I'm with you, honey. I'm with you. I'll always be with you, baby," she whispered. She continued to hold him until he leand back on the couch and used his shirt sleeves to dry his eyes.

"Look after Mrs. Akers," he finally said, "and see her home when she's ready. I have some things to do." He let Tipper in from the cold and put him in the extra bedroom away from the women.

"Be careful. Please, be careful," Missy said as Andy went out the door.

Andy drove to the Prairie Trail Motel where he knew Romme stayed. The red welding truck was gone. The two trucks the workers used were there. He was not going to work today, and he surmised the other men weren't either. The newly fallen snow had brought with it a significant drop in temperature. The town was crawling with cops, sheriff deputies, and agents from the Kansas Bureau of Investigation. It was unlikely anyone would venture out so far as to run across their work site, but if anyone who was a part of the 'top secret' project had anything to do with the bank robbery, they had only themselves to blame for the unwanted attention.

Andy wanted to talk to Buster Warren. He was not at the auto dealership. Andy drove by his house. Neighbors surrounded the place, coming and going, bearing gifts of food. His wife's brother had been murdered. Andy decided not to stop. His cell phone buzzed. It was Police Chief Stevens. The authorities wanted to speak with him, and would he come down to the police station. Andy told the Chief he'd be there in thirty minutes. At first, he was ready and eager to comply with the request. Then he realized they wouldn't ask questions just about him. They were going to want to know what he'd seen about town, what he'd heard, who he'd met.

Officer Bradford met him at the door with a somber, no-nonsense expression. Jason had been his friend, too. He directed Andy to a private room. Two men he'd never met came in, both wearing ties, one with his suit jacket on, the other with his white shirt sleeves rolled up to the elbow. This wasn't going to be a friendly chat over coffee about someone reporting a stolen tractor.

"Mr. Branson, I'm agent Reddick, and this is agent Dudley with the Kansas Bureau of Investigation." We're recording this conversation." He set a hand-held device on the table and switched it on. "Where were you last night?"

"Home, asleep."

"When did you go to bed?"

"It was early for me. I'd say ten. Maybe ten-thirty."

"Did you hear or see anything unusual?"

"No."

"We understand there's new construction going on in town with a lot of workers here that wouldn't otherwise be in Elmwater. Have you met some of these people?" Reddick asked.

"Yes, casually. Haven't gotten to know any of them."

The other agent stepped forward, leaned over, and placed both hands squarely on the table. "Let me ask you straight up, who do you think committed the robbery?"

Andy shook his head. "I have no idea. I've been trying to come up with someone myself. A lot of people knew Mr. Whitmire and knew the layout of the bank, but I don't know anyone who would kill him."

"What else have you heard?"

"What do you mean? I haven't heard anything."

Agent Dudley's face got closer to Andy's. "The people we've talked to say you're a pretty perceptive guy. Nothing gets past you. We even recieved a report you got into a shouting match with our dead banker."

"What? Who told you that?"

"Never mind. Is it true?"

"That was business. Yeah, we had words, but I knew that man all my life. I'd never lay a finger on him."

But you knew the bank was flush with cash. You decided to make your play. Get what was coming to you and hell with everyone else."

Astonishment registered in Andy's eyes. He became so flabbergasted with the accusation, for a moment he couldn't think. "No, I didn't do anything."

Dudley took Andy's hesitation as a crack in his story. "Can anyone confirm your whereabouts last night?"

"No, I told you, I was at home alone sleeping."

"So, you'd have no objection to our searching your house? Or do we need a warrant?"

Andy couldn't believe his ears. "Yeah, yeah if that's what you want. I have nothing to hide."

"Or you could tell us who did it, and save everyone a lot of time."

"I don't know who did it." At that moment, Andy knew he could divulge everything about the work going on at the old missile silo, and get the heat off his back. He could send the cops scurrying after a promising lead, and a productive lead it would most likely be.

It was foolish not to speak up and tell the cops everything he knew. They would get to the bottom of what was going on at the silo and probably have the perpetrators of the bank robbery behind bars in a matter of days. But he knew he wasn't going to do that. He was too stubborn, fool-hardy, call it what you will. He would avenge Jason's death. He would ruin whatever was the goal at the silo. The cops were squeezing him because they hadn't come up with anything to work with from the other people in town. The answers were at the silo, and all along, the 'free money' in town was a diversion, a distraction. He was on the inside now. He would stay close to the rocket and wait.

"You can go, for now, Mr. Branson," Dudley said, "but don't leave town. We may want to talk to you again."

Around the bank were multiple strands of yellow tape. The vehicles Andy passed seemed to be traveling in slow motion. His mind and body were doing the same: a bank robbery and multiple murders in Elmwater. It was hard to fathom. Everything that happened in the last three months was odd, and Andy was sure the reasons for the unusual occurrences were all tied together. He headed back to his house.

Missy anxiously met him at her door. "Are you all right?" she asked.

"A little stressed, that's all. Do I look that bad?" Andy gave her a wink.

"What happened?"

He looked into her caring brown eyes and knew he could never love another woman as much as he loved Missy. Already she was his comfort, and his rock, a willing listener and someone to hold. She was here for him now, and he knew she would always be.

"The cops are interviewing everyone in town. They're squeezing everyone to see if anyone leaks."

"What did they say to you?"

"Don't worry, Sweetie, they're not after me. They raked me over the coals a bit, but no harm."

"So, do they know who did it? Do they have any

good leads?"

"Not yet. Not that I know of. Anyone could have done it. It wouldn't have been that hard to get to Whitmire. Everyone is a suspect. They're going to have to come up with hard evidence before they can narrow down the list."

"I made spaghetti and meatballs. Are you hungry?"

Andy nodded. "Am I ever."

Missy set a plate for him and Ethel. Andy dug into the food as though he hadn't eaten in a week.

"Do you have any idea who may have done this, Mrs. Akers?" Andy asked.

Ethel shook her head and picked at her food. She was no longer crying but remained lost in a state of shock, obviously unable to fathom the events of the morning.

We need to see the bank books if we can," he said. "It might tell a lot about who perpetrated the robbery. The two of you can figure them out. I would imagine all the money coming into town flowed through Whitmire's fingers, so we need to find out where it came from and where it went. Are you with me?"

"I'm with you, Andy," Missy said, "but the authorities will probably look at all of that now." She gave him her heart melting smile. "Still, you should be a detective."

"You think so?" He smiled.

CHAPTER TWENTY-SIX

ANDY LEFT THE HOUSE headed for the motel again in search of Romme. First, he stopped by the post office for his regular mail. In his box was a note he had a certified letter he could sign for it at the counter. The contents was a summons to appear in the district court in Bridgedale at 10:00 a.m. on February 1st. It included a formal document of the lawsuit:

THOMPSON
VRS
BRANSON

After the initial letter back in November, Andy had a lawyer handle the details. Now he had to make an appearance in court within a month. Andy could only sigh. The first bank robbery in Elmwater's history, his best friend murdered, an unexplained missing man from the work site, a rocket being built outside of town, and now a lawsuit that could easily bankrupt him. What a great way to start the new year.

MENDENHALL AWOKE EARLY and dressed quickly. A sixth sense told him something was amiss. Maybe his subconscious had heard all the vehicles that rushed into town during the early morning hours. Their sirens were silent, but a flood of emergency strobe lights had lit up his motel room curtains with colors pulsating off the walls. He hadn't slept well. He put on a coat and went to warm up his car.

Romme's truck wasn't in the parking lot. He drove to the grocery store, bought a large coffee, and listened carefully as Mae Morgan filled in a gathering of customers on the overnight events. There had been a bank robbery overnight, and two men killed. The perpetrators were still at large. Blood drained from Mendenhall's face, and he felt a hollow ache in the pit of his stomach. He slipped out of the grocery store, threw his coffee cup on the sidewalk, and rushed to his car.

The bank was wrapped in yellow tape. Mendenhall drove by the police station and saw more cars than he could count surrounding the building. Everything he wanted to avoid was happening. The town was going to get as much attention as a forty car pileup on the interstate. Newspaper reporters from larger towns in the area would start snooping around. If their work on the military property wasn't discovered, it would be a stroke of pure luck. But they would be discovered. There was one farm boy who would spill his guts as soon as the authorities asked him a single question. All would be lost. Mendenhall had to deal with Andy, and now.

Mendenhall returned to the motel and knocked on Hanania and Raghib's door. The men were getting ready to go to work, but Mendenhall told them to take the day off. The workers in the other rooms were informed to sleep in. There was fresh snow on the ground; the weather had turned bitter cold.

"The local bank got robbed last night and two people killed," he said. "The town's already buzzing with cops. We've got to stay away from the site until things quiet down. The snowfall will help us there, I think. It should cover our tracks onto the property. We have a loose end to take care of in the meantime – the local farmer who's been working at the site. He knows too much, and he has seen too much. If the cops question him, he'll spill his guts for sure, and we're dead."

Hanania and Raghib listened to his every word and knew what he meant. They had come too far to get derailed now. Whatever Mendenhall had in mind, they would assist in every way they could. Hanania was close to seventy years of age and not up to what Mendenhall had in mind. But Raghib could do the job. He was in his mid-thirties, strong, an experienced assassin, and dedicated to Islam. The farmer had to be located and made to disappear. Raghib had worked alongside Andy for more than a month and would know him by sight. Mendenhall gave him the two addresses where he most likely would be.

"He has to be silenced," Mendenhall said. "Get him in your truck if you can, and take care of him outside of town. If he doesn't get in with you, ask him to follow you. Maybe he'll want to tell you what he knows about the robbery. Just find him, and get rid of him. Don't stop looking for him until you do."

"Have either of you seen Romme since yesterday?" Mendenhall asked.

The other two men shook their heads. Mendenhall dismissed the question from his mind as soon as he asked it. There were more important details to attend to now, and he wanted Raghib on Andy's trail immediately.

Raghib was a man of few words. He obeyed superiors and efficiently performed his work. He was next to invisible because of his unquestioning attitude. When necessary, he was a silent serpent who dealt death with little more than a whimper from his victims. Whatever the assignment, Raghib was efficient and unquestioning.

But when it came to specific tactics, Raghib took his own counsel. As the white van warmed, he considered the best way to approach Andy to get close to him. If he killed him in the country, there would be no way to bury him. His body would be laying in the open for anyone to see. However, if he killed him at his farmhouse, it might be days before someone found his body. Raghib considered a way to make his death make sense to authorities. He trudged back through the snow to Mendenhall's motel room.

"Do you have any cash?" he asked once inside the room.

"Some. What's it for?"

"You want the man dead, right? It's for a set-up to keep the cops off our tail. How much do you have?

"I have plenty of cash. You don't need to worry about how much."

"Okay then, how about five thousand in a bag, preferably some that still have paper wrappers. If this guy's found dead with a bulk of cash, the cops might think he was part of the robbery, and his cohorts took him out to keep him quiet."

Mendenhall smiled and began packing a small leather bag.

Back in the van, Raghib drove toward the center of town. On Peach Street, he found the address, but no pick-up. He left the residential area, headed north. Raghib spied the truck he was looking for as it pulled into the city hall parking lot. He waited for Andy to park, then stopped behind his truck and rolled down the window.

"Hey, I'm headed out. You want a ride? Save two trucks plowing through the snow." Raghib drew a .45 pistol from his waistband and held it with his right hand in his lap.

Andy knew who called to him and he didn't trust him any more than Mendenhall or Romme. "I can't go out today," he said as he approached the van. "Things have happened in town that need my help."

Raghib recycled the pistol in his lap, an unmistakable sound. Andy froze. "Move an inch, and this gun will knock a hole in this door that will blow right through you," Raghib said. "Come here and get in the driver's seat. We need to have a little talk." As Andy walked forward, Raghib scooted over in the seat. When Andy was inside, Raghib told him to drive to his farmhouse.

"What do you want?" Andy said, his eyes focused ahead. "You probably know about the bank robbery. Well, the cops have already talked to me, and I didn't tell them a thing." He drove the long way to his house. He doubted this guy knew where he lived, and he prayed the women weren't still there.

"Just keep driving."

Andy drove east across town, then doubled back, headed northwest on another street where it intersected Main again, and he turned north. "Listen," Andy said, "whatever errand you're on, you and your boss got it all wrong. I haven't said a word. You do something to me, and the town's going to crawl with more police. Take me back to my truck. I told your boss I'd be quiet, and I am." Andy saw Missy's car in the drive. His heart sank, and he kept driving.

"Stop." Raghib hollered. 'This is your place. There aren't any more houses up that way. Besides, it says right there on the fence – BRANSON HAULING. You stu-ped American. Back up, and drive in there."

As he turned to look behind to back up the road, Andy got a good look at Raghib. The three words he had spoken brought complete clarity to Andy's mind. He needed no more answers. The missing pieces of logic and motivation were now in perfect focus, all in an instant. The reasons for free money in town and secret work on the abandoned military property all made sense.

Until now, Andy had thought he would show up his neighbors and prove to them the 'government grant' was all a fraud. He would show them, teach them that he was smarter than the whole bunch tied together. They wouldn't second guess him again. They wouldn't treat him like an oversized child who's opinions weren't worth the time of day.

The rocket was more than a test, which he always suspected, but now he was truly frightened. Its purpose was to create widespread devastation. This matter was no longer about getting one over on the guys at the diner. This was about life and death. The thought of what they planned to put in the nose cone of the rocket sent shivers up his spine. If he got away from Raghib, should he take Missy and run?

The engine sections were assembled. How long would it take to attach the nose cone and launch the thing? Raghib and his superiors were in a panic about something, in all likelihood the bank robbery, but that didn't mean they couldn't finish their plan. Andy was confused and afraid with a .45 pointed at his ribs as he pulled into the driveway and parked in front of his house.

Raghib followed Andy inside, the gun in his coat pocket. Tipper was sleeping under the coffee table. Missy had let him out from the back room. The dog always made a commotion when locked away when people were around. Missy was housecleaning.

With a wad of tissues still in her hands, Ethel listened to a gaggle of women on TV sit around a table, and talk about nothing.

Raghib was pleased to see the young woman. "Tie them up," Raghib demanded as he pulled the gun into view.

"Andy?" Missy's face went pale.

"Do what he says, baby. It'll be all right."

Raghib stepped to the kitchen counter and cut the electrical cords from the toaster and a mixer. "Tie her ankles together and her hands behind her back."

Ethel turned toward the kitchen and watched the scene in stark horror. Andy bound Missy's ankles together and her hands behind her back. Raghib checked the knots and wasn't satisfied. "You have any cord or rope?"

"Yes."

"Where is it?"

"Out in the shed."

"Andy, it already hurts."

Raghib fired a shot across the room that smashed into the far wall and backhanded Missy across the face. "Shut up, bitch."

Before the words were out of his mouth, Tipper flew into the Arab and bit down on his gun hand. The dog's aim couldn't have been better. Raghib screamed and dropped the gun. Andy grabbed him in a chokehold, and flung his legs into the wall, threw him on the floor and dropped a knee into his face. All the while, the dog ripped at his hand.

Andy grabbed the .45 off the floor and untied Missy's hands.

"Get the rope off the back porch," he said.

Missy unbound her feet and was quick to the task. Andy took the rope and gave her the gun. "It's ready to fire. Keep it on him but don't pull the trigger unless he moves. That thing can put a hole through a concrete wall."Andy bound Raghib's feet faster than a cowboy could tie down a calf. Blood oozed from the corner of Raghib's mouth. His teeth were red. Andy flipped him over and tied his hands. Andy finished by duct taping his mouth and using a kitchen towel to blindfold him.

"Watch him, Tipper." The dog's muscles went taut, and he growled. Tipper would take a chunk out of the man's ear if he so much as flinched.

Andy took the two women down the hall. Missy was sobbing and clung to him. Ethel walked one stiff step after another as though she were in a trance. He pulled them into the bedroom, sat Missy on the bed, and found a chair for Ethel, and concocted a lie on the fly.

"Mrs. Akers, I don't want you to worry about this. This has nothing to do with what happened to Mr. Whitmire, so I'm asking you not to talk about it." He looked into her eyes. "This was just a misunderstanding that got out of hand with a guy and me over in Salina. I'm going to take this guy back and dump him on his boss's porch. They're trying to intimidate me, and it won't work." He patted her hand. "Will you be okay if we take you back to your car?"

"I'll be all right. I need to go home," Ethel said.

Before they left, Andy put Raghib on his stomach, looped a rope around his neck that ran under his tied hands, bent his legs at the knees and tied the ends of the rope to his ankles. If he tried to extend his legs, he'd choke himself.

After they took Ethel home, they drove to city hall to get his truck. Andy told her everything he knew.

"Baby, I'm going to need your help. I'm sure the easy money in town, the bank robbery, and the project I've been working on up north of town are all tied together. First, we have to get rid of the scumbag at the house. "I'm thinking, throw him in the van and take him to Salina and abandon the truck there. It may take several days for someone to find him, but he'll survive. He has on a heavy coat. You follow me and wait at one of the truck stops on the interstate. I'll call you and tell you where to pick me up."

With a plan in place, they drove back to the farm. As soon as they were near enough to see the drive, a hollow ache rolled in Andy's guts. The van was gone. Andy had Missy turn her car around and wait, ready to flee if Andy encountered trouble. He had the gun in his pocket, and he fingered it nervously as he stepped on the porch.

He opened the front door to an empty house. Raghib was gone, his bindings strewn over the kitchen floor. All the tools and mail from the kitchen table were scattered. Tipper scampered into the living room, whimpering. Andy knelt beside the dog and stroked him. He had a red mark on his forehead but otherwise seemed unhurt. The house was vacant and silent. Raghib had gotten away, and he and his cohorts would still be waiting to grab Andy the first chance they got.

CHAPTER TWENTY-SEVEN

A COUPLE OF DETECTIVES came by the motel, flashed badges at Mendenhall and asked questions about who he was, who he was with, and what he was doing in town. Mendenhall told them he and his men were part of the construction team working on the new grain elevator. The answers apparently satisfied the cops as they hadn't been back. Either they didn't compare notes with other detectives back at police headquarters, or they figured anyone associated with the robbery wasn't sitting around town. Twelve days until the launch; Mendenhall swallowed another handful of Tums.

Mendenhall was glad he and Hanania had tailed Raghib around town while he was looking for Andy. They drove past the drive and waited on the north side of the farmhouse when the men went inside. Mendenhall and Hanania approached the house from the back, ready to help Raghib finish the job. But when Andy and the two women left the house, they went inside to see what had happened. They found Raghib hogtied, helpless, and whining. Hanania cut him free. The men raced back into town in the two vans.

THE NEXT DAY, ASIM AND HIS TEAM drove into Elmwater in the middle of the night. Romme was with them. They didn't go near the town and accessed the site by way of the Davis' farm. The men from Kansas City drove one large Ryder truck with the rocket nose cone, and two fully assembled atomic bombs in a van. Hazy dawn peeked over the eastern horizon as they arrived at the site. Within minutes the sun burnt away the morning mist and sunlight reflected brilliantly off the snow-covered prairie.

A fully assembled rocket engine was in the silo. Steel arms, welded into the silo walls, held the rocket steady in a vertical position. A ½ inch thick steel plate bolted over the top of the engine protected the solid fuel from precipitation.

The nose cone was maneuvered into place and held in position as it was aligned, then bolted to the rocket frame. The bomb, ignition bubble switch, high-amperage marine battery, six dynamite belts, and a directional gyro rested on a 3 X 3-foot platform of hard rubber. An asbestos sheet was glued over the steel plate, and the bomb assembly bolted to it. The bubble switch was kept open with a wooden insert to prevent mishaps before launch. The neutron deflector remained between the two uranium half shells.

One ton in weight, the nose cone was seven feet long and five feet in diameter and opened and closed like a hatch. For the launch, eight locking bolts would secure it into the top steel plate. During preparations, its twenty-inch hinge could be swung open and closed with the help of the hydraulic lift still stretched over the mouth of the silo. Ceramic tiles had been secured with industrial epoxy over the outer surface of the nose cone as a reentry heat shield, and the exterior surface painted black.

The men worked throughout the day and into the night. Asim watched as they lowered the bomb onto the base plate. It was delicate work as the holes in the rubber base had to match the holes in the steel plate. A single slip and a tool or chain might hit the assembly and damage a critical component. The whole damn thing might fall into the silo, and all would be lost. When the bomb assembly was secure, Asim inspected everything with the care of a brain surgeon removing a tumor. Everything was in place. The bomb was ready to fly. The nose cone was closed, but not bolted. All that remained were the final inputs before locking down the nose cone right before launch. When the warhead was ready, it was only nine days until launch.

The weather in Washington in the third week of January was forecast to be clear and dry with temperatures in the high forties. The annual State of the Union Address was a regular event. Politicians gathered to praise or ignore the President's comments as fit their whims, usually along party lines. But most importantly, whatever their reasons for attending, they would be there.

AFTER THE ATTEMPT ON HIS LIFE, Andy had no more questions. Now he had to act. The generous grant of money to the town was nothing but a distracting ruse. The rocket was being built to destroy and kill. He didn't need to know its target or its payload. All he knew was that it could never blast off from that ancient silo.

For several days, Andy worked on a plan to sabotage the rocket in the middle of the night. He would have to work in the dark with no one to lower him in a harness deep into the silo. All the while, he was continually vigilant of his property. He walked around the shed every fifteen minutes looking in every direction. If he heard a vehicle approaching, he grabbed a shotgun. They would not catch him by surprise. If any of Mendenhall's men came after him, they'd face three 12-gauge shotguns, fully loaded with six shells each plus Raghib's .45 caliber pistol of which Andy was becoming increasingly fond.

Andy made the trip to Concordia and talked to the owner of a tree trimming company. He bought a tree climbing sling and paid extra to learn how to use it. By attaching the apparatus to the cables strung across the silo opening, he could lower himself forty feet.

After midnight, he headed across the prairie on the four-wheeler at five miles an hour, lights off, the dog remained at the house. Tipper was good at being quiet, but he couldn't afford even a muffled growl if the dog heard or sensed someone else at the site. And someone else would be there. Andy knew there would be at least one guard near the rocket. When he'd covered at least four miles, Andy shut down the four-wheeler and continued on foot with the tree climbing gear, metal shears, three strands of 4-foot clothesline cord, and the .45 caliber pistol.

The cold night could knock down a city dweller in a matter of minutes, but Andy was used to it. Bundled head to toe, Andy focused on his mission. The sharp winter air kept his mind clear. Step by step, he trudged through the snow, more than a mile further to the site. And with each step, he was more determined than ever to see his plan through.

The moon was but a narrow silver sickle in the sky, but the sky was clear, and an array of stars lit his path reflecting off the crystal snow. He saw the cargo containers in the distance, the semi-tractor, and a panel truck and a van. He turned so that his approach would be from behind the equipment.

Andy knelt beside a cargo container and listened. He heard nothing but the gentle rustle of the breeze through the high grass. He watched for a flashlight or movement of any kind across the flat terrain. There was nothing. He had to find the guard and subdue him before he dare lower himself into the hole. But if the guard were sleeping in one of the vehicles, he had no idea how to wake him and maintain the upper hand. He could point his weapon at the guard, but to tie him up, he'd have to lay the gun aside.

Limestone rocks were plentiful, and he threw

one against the back of the panel truck. Nothing happened. He threw another rock, and when silence was the only response, Andy slowly opened the driver side door and found it empty. Next, he threw stones at the door panels of the semi-tractor, fully expecting someone to jump from the cab. Nothing happened. All the doors on the van were locked. He paced around the work site. Tonight it was unguarded. Tonight he was alone.

Andy moved to the hole and unslung the tree climbing gear. He fastened two clamps on the support cable across the hole and slipped into the harness. Hand over hand, he pulled himself over the hole until he was even with the side of the rocket engine, then he let himself down into the silo. He maneuvered around the rocket until he found one of the tubes that ran up the side. With heavy gauge metal shears, the kind used to break chains and locks, Andy cut the tube in two. He didn't know if it held the ignition cables or rocket controls. It didn't matter. He intended to cut them both. To make sure the first tube was completely severed, Andy sliced the tube again an inch below the first cut. He was hopeful no one would decend low enough to see the damage.

He stuck the shears in the ammo pouch of his pants and pulled himself around to the other side of the rocket. He was about to sever the other tube when a blinding light shown down from above. Andy was startled. Involuntarily, he snapped up a huge breath. He was caught and defenseless. Demonic laughter rolled down the silo walls and engulfed him.

"You stu-ped American. I thought it was you."

It was Raghib. Andy would never forget that voice.

"I was in the back of the truck," he said. "You didn't look there. So stu-ped." Again, the laughter came, deep, heartfelt, a belly laugh with all the sinister inflections of a human predator who had his victim cornered.

Andy heard the snap of a knife opening. A side brace that kept the rocket vertical was a yard above him. He pulled himself up on the I-beam right before one of the ropes dropped loosely on his head. Andy grabbed the .45 from his waistband and emptied the clip toward the shadow that blocked starlight at the top of the hole. Several rounds zinged off metal. But at least one hit the mark. Raghib let out a grunt, fell into the hole, bounced off a beam, and hit the blast floor with a thud. A split second later, Andy heard an unmistakable splash deep in the bowels of the silo.

He scooted along the beam to the criss-cross of girders embedded in the silo wall. One rope remained attached to his harness. At least he had a safety line, but he couldn't pull himself up with one rope. His only way out was to scale the maze of girders in the wall, but at the moment he was in total darkness. Andy leaned against the silo wall to catch his breath and dropped the shears into the depths to get rid of the weight. He had no choice but to start climbing.

By pulling himself up to the diagonal beams, he was able to scale the wall. When he reached the center point where beams crossed, he took up the slack in his rope to cinch up his safety line. Every ten feet he reached one of the lateral beams used to keep the rocket vertical. He could pull himself up to the next level and begin the struggle once again. Forty feet seemed such a short distance, and it was unless you were going straight up. Andy lost track of time. But before long, the early dawn began to cast a sliver of light over the lip of the silo. He had to get out before Mendenhall, and his men came. If they found him anywhere near the silo, he was a dead man.

He had one more ten-foot section of wall to scale. His forearms ached, his fingers were numb. Finally, he made it to the surface and fell prostrate on the ground outside the hole. He rested no more than twenty seconds before he pulled his single rope across the support cable and unbuckled both clamps, removed his harness, and dropped all the gear so that it fell past the blast floor and into the water below. A quick look around proved he was still alone. He headed across the snow-covered prairie, his face pressed into the brisk morning wind, toward his four-wheeler as fast as he could move.

CHAPTER TWENTY-EIGHT

R OMME'S MIND WAS PREOCCUPIED No one asked him about the bank robbery. Mendenhall had chewed him out good for disappearing for three days, but if he had any suspicions, he kept them to himself. The fact that the bank robbery happened only made Mendenhall and Asim more anxious about the launch, and the prospect of being discovered. Romme's unexplained absence was a distraction, but Mendenhall and Asim remained focused on the goal.

After the launch, Romme was to receive his final payment in the form of a wad of bills and would be expected to disappear. He planned to head back to Jersey. In and around New York City was an ideal place to make good use of a lot of loose cash.

Asim gave Romme the keys to the panel truck that had been kept locked and hidden behind the sandstone bluff since the day it arrived. At two in the morning, he and two other men drove into town. It took them three hours to complete a new assignment. Romme perspired in spite of the cold, physically tired, and mentally exhausted. The three men drove to the motel.

Before he got to his door, Mendenhall opened his and summoned him.

"Any problems?" Mendenhall spoke in a cautious, breathless voice. He had been up all night waiting for an update. He still had on his pants. His hair was disheveled. The coffee pot was half full.

"No problems."

Mendenhall's brain searched for any detail left undone. "The receiver is on?"

"It's on. We did everything according to Asim's instructions. Now I've done my work. I want to get paid and get out of here," Romme said.

"You know the arrangement. Besides, I don't have it all now. A few more days," Mendenhall replied.

Romme stood with his back against the motel wall and with one powerful thrust of his leg smashed the heel of his boot through it. "I don't like being strung along. I thought we worked together well, and I have no problem helping you achieve your goals. But I expect to be paid. It's not going to end well if I'm not."

"Go to bed," Mendenhall said. "You're getting all worked up for nothing. I'll pay you as soon as I get all the cash. You won't have to wait 'till the launch."

Romme slept in the next morning, then ate a breakfast of Pringles and black coffee in his room. A shower made him feel better. He was not happy about having to hang around town, but he could endure it. Part of him wanted to stick around, be twenty miles down the road next Monday and see the firey exhaust of the rocket launch. Another part of him wanted to be a hundred miles east of Kansas City already.

He went to the grocery store for something decent to eat. He purposefully avoided the diner, and the Dairy Queen wasn't open. He sat in his truck, eating powdered donuts and an energy drink. The bank still had yellow tape around it. Maybe he should leave. His take at the bank was close to fifty grand. He wanted the money Mendenhall owed him, but maybe he shouldn't push it. In one sense, the money he stole was Al-Qaeda money anyway. Without Mendenhall's huge injection into the local economy, the bank wouldn't have near that much cash on hand. From what he gathered from Mendenhall, the city had received around twenty million dollars in total. If the plan were successfully pulled off, Al-Quaeda would consider all the money well spent.

Even Mendenhall didn't know where Romme lived back in Jersey. The only way Mendenhall got in touch with him was through a mailbox in Newark that he'd set up under an assumed name. Romme knew he would never go back to that mailbox for any reason. He should go to Kansas City, pick up the money, drive to St Louis and dump the truck, and buy another vehicle. That was the smart move. The authorities would never find him. This concocted jihadist scheme may not work out as planned, but something devastating was going to happen. The further away he was from all of it, the better off he'd be.

But he wanted the money Mendenhall owed him. $25,000 was too much money to ignore. He would wait a few more hours, then find out if more money had come in today. He had $25,000 coming to him, and he intended to collect.

The day was bright, bright as a winter day could be. The air was calm. Winter on the plains held its breath and wrapped itself in a blanket of cold. The wind abated for a time, replaced by a crisp chill huddled over the landscape. Until the heavy snows or blizzards came, Mother Nature was at peace. Deep breaths of fresh air instantly invigorated the body and soul. There was something spiritual about winter on the prairie.

Romme drove back to the motel. Mendenhall's car was not in the lot. But the other men were looking for him and wanted the truck he was driving so they could head back to Kansas City. Romme was willing to give up the van, but someone needed to take him to the site to get his welding truck. At the site, all was well. He turned over the van, collected his tools, and was back in town in less than an hour. He knew Mendenhall and Asim were waiting for the exact moment to launch. But the longer he waited, the more agitated he became. The other men were gone, and he was stuck, twiddling his thumbs.

By mid-afternoon Romme was going crazy looking at the motel room ceiling, so he headed to Fred's Tavern. The place was as dank, dusty, and dark as he'd remembered, although Fred may have put on a clean undershirt. Some kid who looked underage was playing a pinball machine. A middle-aged Mexican couple was talking, nursing their beers at a corner table. Romme ordered a draft and turned his back to the bar and stared at the brick wall above the front door.

"A dollar fifty," Fred said.

"You got any peanuts?"

Fred pointed to a candy machine. Romme looked it over. Nothing but chocolate and caramel, M&M's and Skittles, but no peanuts. Romme drank his beer. As he was about to order another, three men walked in the bar.

Romme was surprised to see them, but the men's body language and cockeyed grins indicated they knew he was there.

"Well, if it isn't the dumbass looking for the employment office."

"Don't start any shit, Roy," Fred said, as he smacked his hand on the bar. Romme was startled and amused. Fred did have blood pressure. The old codger pointed at Roy, "if you don't have anything better to do, just leave."

"Fred relax. We need three beers."

Fred maintained the scowl and opened three bottles. The man Romme hadn't seen before went to the bar and got the beers.

"Your pretty little waitress there could have brought those over if she wanted a tip," Roy said while looking at his friends.

"I don't think she's that pretty," said another man. "She'd have to pay me." The comment made little sense, but the three laughed anyway.

"Well, I'm damn sure prettier than your girlfriends, Roy," Romme said.

Instantly, Roy threw a bottle of beer at Romme, hitting him in the leg. The other two pushed their chairs back. One pulled a club from his pant leg. They surrounded Romme, backing him toward the bar.

"I'm calling the cops," screamed Fred.

Romme remained still, adrenalin powering his body, instinct and training plotting his first move. The man with the club approached on his right. When he got close, Romme feined a left hook and caught him in the jaw with a spinning kick. The man parried the kick a bit with his left arm, but Romme followed with a left cross to his face. The man staggered back. Roy threw a punch that got blocked. The other man poured his beer on the floor and took a swing at his head with the empty bottle. Romme ducked just in time.

The first man was back in the fight. One of them grabbed Romme by the shirt. Another got in a punch to his gut. Romme kicked one of them in the groin, and the man crumpled to the floor. Romme took out Roy with a flurry of one-two punches that turned his mouth and nose into a bloody fountain. The other guy threw a barstool at Romme that caught him in the side, then bounced off the brick wall. Romme moved toward him, and the man fled for the front door. Romme caught his breath. He'd taken a couple blows, but he'd been through worse. A minute later, two cops walked through the door.

"Arrest 'um. Arrest 'um all," shouted Fred. "They tore up my place."

"They started it, officer. I was only protecting myself," Romme said.

Roy had a bandana in his hand, soaking up his bloody face. "Looks like you picked on someone your own size this time, Roy. Come' on. You too, Spencer. And you too, mister. Hands behind your back," said the police officer.

"They jumped me," Romme protested.

"Yeah well, the judge gets paid the big bucks to listen to your side of the story," the cop said as he snapped cuffs on Romme's wrists.

CHAPTER TWENTY-NINE

ROMME AWOKE THE NEXT MORNING battered and bruised. He made his allowed phone call to Mendenhall, who said little. There was a good chance Mendenhall would do nothing. The clock was ticking. Mendenhall had priorities other than him.

"Let me out." Romme's head throbbed. Those plow boys at the bar had been looking for him. He made them pay, but they got him good. They had brought along an extra friend to help them handle what they couldn't handle on their own.

"Shut up," yelled a man from the other end of the row of cells. They'd all been arrested for disorderly conduct and disturbing the peace. Romme didn't care if the other men had gotten off. It was his hide he was worried about. He was in big trouble stuck behind bars.

"Who's out there? Talk to me." The cell house was gloomy, a view of gray cinder blocks and grayer bars. "I have to talk to someone." He took off his boot and beat a continuous thud on the bars. "I have to talk to someone."

Finally, a deputy came down the hall.

"What's your problem, mister? If you don't like the accommodations, you'll have to take it up with the maid."

"I want to post bail."

"Judge is at the county seat. That's where the court is. He only comes 'round twice a month, and he was here last week."

"No. He can't make me wait that long. I've got rights. I want to post bail."

"If you've got a lawyer. Maybe he could speed things up for you."

"What day is this?"

"The 16th. It's Wednesday, yeah the 16th," said the jailer.

"No, no. I got to get out of here. I want to call a lawyer."

"You had your phone call. You need to sit back and relax."

The deputy turned to walk away. Romme reached for him through the bars. The deputy jumped back and hit his arm with a nightstick.

"Please. I'm begging you. Let me talk to the chief. Let me call a lawyer. I got to get out of here."

"The chief's out of town till Saturday. You're going to be right here until at least then."

"Why?" Romme pleaded. I didn't do nothing."

The deputy laughed. "Drunk and disorderly. No wonder you don't remember anything. You busted Fred's up good. I saw it."

"I wasn't drunk. I got jumped."

The deputy shrugged his shoulders.

"I got to get out of here I tell you. Hey, you know that Andy fellow for sure. I had him working for me. Call him up. Call him, please. Have him visit me. That's the least you can do. Will you? Just give him a call."

For the next two days, Romme constantly screamed with the conviction of a wolf howling at the moon. He beat on the bars and threw things around his cell. When he was exhausted, he rested for ten minutes, then began his tirade all over again. On Saturday, the chief came in to see him. The result was that he was staying put. The chief said he couldn't do anything until he first saw the judge.

Under his breath, he cursed Mendenhall. Mendenhall was going to let him sit and endure the fate of the town. He wanted to scream to the sky what he knew, throw a wrench into the plans the Jihadist had worked four months to put in motion. But he dared not. To admit what he knew meant he'd never go free. The authorities would likely link him to the bank the longer he stayed in jail. Andy was his only hope. The deputy said he'd given him a call. He had to get that gullible farmer to do what he suggested.

On Sunday afternoon, Andy walked in, accompanied by a deputy. Romme stood and hugged the bars. Andy saw the strain on Romme's face, but also the relief as though his presence was the embodiment of an angel.

"Can we talk in private," Romme asked the guard in a tone of voice as though he were a child asking a teacher for a hall pass.

The guard pulled a chair from across the walkway. "You got privacy. Ten minutes." Then he walked down the row of cells and sat in front of the door leading to the office.

Romme squatted near the floor of his cell still clinging to the bars. "You gotta get me out of here, today, he whispered.

"Today's Sunday. I can't do anything for you today," Andy replied.

"Oh my god. Monday. Monday. Tomorrow, tomorrow," he sounded like a madman. "You've got to get me out tomorrow morning."

"How?"

"Get a lawyer to see the judge at your county seat. Get him to set bail. It can't be that hard. Pay the bail. It can't be that much. I'm in here for a bar fight I didn't start. Pay the bail. They'll let me out."

Andy listened but knew he'd be lucky to get all that done in two days, much less before noon tomorrow. "I don't know. All before noon? I doubt it."

Romme clung to the bars like a man sinking in quicksand. He lowered his head and whispered at the floor. "They're going to launch the rocket tomorrow evening."

"Tomorrow, huh? You sure? When exactly?"

"Around 7:00, P.M"

Andy wasn't surprised. Still, a bolt of panic passed through him all the same. "I thought you said it was a military test? Why would it be launched at night?"

"Forget all that," Romme pleaded. "You've got to stop them."

"What? Stop them? How many people will be there?"

"I'm not sure, but not many. Two or three. Maybe half a dozen. Maybe only one."

"How am I supposed to stop them?"

Romme looked up. Beads of sweat glistened along his hairline. His eyes were sharp and clear. His breathing was choppy, sucking air like a child getting over a cry. "You're going to have to kill them," he uttered, barely above a whisper.

Andy looked at him for a moment and instantly knew it was true. Romme meant it. Andy knew he had disabled the rocket but had he really? Raghib had stopped him from cutting the second cable tube. What if his sabotage had been discovered in the last few days and the damage repaired? Andy had prayed the rocket was rendered harmless. Now he was sick with doubt. He knew he had already killed one man. Andy sat back, gazed high on the cell bars, and took a deep breath. He stood transfixed hearing Romme's words echo in his brain.

"Times up," came a voice from the hallway door.

Andy jumped and hurried to the door. "Listen, Bob, this is important. I need a few more minutes, okay? I wouldn't ask otherwise. Just a little longer." The deputy nodded. For once a local connection got him a needed concession. He walked back to Romme's cell.

Andy stared fiercely through the bars. "I don't

want to do that."

"It'll be the only way to stop them" Romme speech was rapid, the words filled with panic. "They're terrorists. You can't call in the state cops either. You have to do it yourself."

"Why?"

"If they see squad cars or they get surrounded they'll blow everything sky high before anyone can get close."

"How am I supposed to go about this?"

"You met Mendenhall. He's in town, so I'm pretty sure he'll be there. He knows who you are, so he shouldn't be surprised you'd show up. Take my AR–15. It has thirty rounds in the clip. Behind my truck seat is a 9MM too. The clip's full. It holds fifteen. They'll have an SUV for a getaway car. In the back will be a large battery to provide the spark to ignite the rocket. But one of them, this is very important, will have a remote transmitter. You've got to find it and take it apart. Smash it if you have to."

"A transmitter? You just said they'd have a battery for ignition."

"Call it a backup. Destroy it. It's the size of a walkie-talkie. You'll know when you find it."

"What if they fire the rocket ahead of time?'

"They won't. 7:00 p.m. tomorrow. 7:00 p.m., no earlier."

"What if they shoot before I get close?"

"Then hide behind your vehicle and use the rifle. But I doubt that will happen. They won't have any long-range weapons."

"And if I'm able to park close?"

"Talk it up. Tell whoever's there you've come to see the fireworks. They'll be glad to let you see the launch. They won't be surprised to see you there. But they won't let you leave alive. Too much risk. They won't let you go."

"So, I'm supposed to shoot them in cold blood?"

Romme gave him an expression where Andy could feel the revulsion in Romme's eyes. "These are not innocent men. If it suited their purpose, they would take a baby from its mother's arms and kill it in front of her. As soon as you get close, you must kill the man with the detonator wires. Then turn your pistol on the rest. And find the transmitter. It must be destroyed."

CHAPTER THIRTY

ANDY LEFT THE JAIL and drove to Missy's apartment. She was on the couch, holding her legs tightly with her chin on her knees. The climax scene of a mystery movie was on the TV. She was absorbed in the outcome. He got a soda from the fridge, sat at a table, and waited for the movie to end.

Andy found it difficult to contemplate the shooting of a man at close range. He didn't want to do that. He didn't want to shoot anybody. 7:00 p.m. tomorrow. He knew every second until then was going to feel like an eternity. He was absorbed in his thoughts when Missy turned to him. "Hi, baby," she said with a smile. The TV was off. She stretched on the couch, then came over to him, and rubbed his back. "Get everything taken care of?"

"I want you to leave town." He stood and gazed into her questioning eyes. "Today. Get your stuff and go to Wichita. Plan to stay for a week." He gently grabbed her shoulders. "Listen, you know how dangerous things are getting around here. I don't want you to get hurt. I don't want a repeat of what happened at the house."

"Where did you go this afternoon?"

"No more questions. I want you to be safe."

"Are you coming with me?"

"I have to stay here."

"Andy, you're scaring me."

He pulled her close and rubbed his cheek in her hair. "Don't be scared, baby. No one's going to hurt you. And no one is going to hurt me. I need you to go – for my peace of mind. I'll call you every day." He carried her to the couch, and quietly, they held each other.

After she said she'd leave tomorrow as soon as she could, he went home. The falling darkness brought a sense of foreboding to his thoughts. He tried to sleep but couldn't. His brain wouldn't rest. He got up and gazed out a back window where far in the distance an armed rocket sat hidden in the ground.

THE NEXT DAY, MONDAY THE 21st of January, Gregory Mendenhall sat in his room at the Prairie Trail Motel drinking strong tea and watching the news on TV. The last two workers still at the motel would drive his car and his belongings back to Kansas City. Asim and Hanania would come to his room within the hour. They had been the brains behind building the rocket and the warhead. They insisted upon seeing the launch. Shortly after two, a light rap came at the motel door. The men entered, and each kissed Mendenhall. He offered them tea, and they each took a chair.

"All looks well," Mendenhall said, pointing at the TV. "We need to leave here in half an hour. It takes a while to get to the site, and we need plenty of time for final preparations." Hanania stretched out on the bed. Asim watched the TV intently listening for updates on their topic of interest.

Mendenhall punched in a number on the motel phone. "A bit of unfinished business I need to take care of."

"Warren Automotive," a receptionist answered.

"I want totest drive a truck you have on the lot, but I won't be able to get over there until after six. Can I see Mr. Warren later today?"

"I'm sorry, but Mr. Warren is out of town. He went to Topeka and won't be back until Wednesday. Can someone else help you?"

Mendenhall clenched the receiver. Anger boiled within him so quickly his face felt hot. "No, no." He hung up. " Just what I was afraid of. Someone who knows too much is going to get away, and I owe that bastard."

"What happened?" Asim asked.

"Oh, this guy gave me the runaround, one of the city councilmen. He's out of town. He's going to be alive after tonight. I wanted to go over to his business and slit his throat.

"Forget him," Asim insisted. "We have more important things to do."

"He knows all about me. He'll be able to put everything together and have the Feds on our tail in no time." Mendenhall stared down the other two men while he inhaled deeply. "There's one other guy who knows too much. I'm going to make sure we get him this time, and I know how to do it."

The three men got in the SUV and drove over to Peach Street where they parked in a short drive beside a small apartment complex. Mendenhall outlined a plan as they drove. They would all approach the door as officials. If she didn't open the door, they'd break it in. Mendenhall knocked on Apt.#4, on the ground level. Missy answered after two knocks, not expecting the malevolence that awaited her. Mendenhall rushed in as soon as she opened the door. Inside, they gagged and tied her hands and feet and hustled her into their SUV.

Mendenhall, Asim, and Hanania drove to the main highway just south of town and turned west. Mendenhall had one last call to make on his cell phone and dialed Andy's number he'd gotten from Romme. The phone rang several times, and Andy answered.

"Andy, this is Mendenhall. We're running a test tonight at the silo. Thought you'd want to see it. Didn't know if you knew. I wanted to call so you could come and see the result of all your hard work. Your girlfriend is here. She wanted to see it real bad."

Andy pulled the phone from his ear and looked at it in his hand. In an instant, blood drained to his feet. Missy didn't leave town like she said she would. Why? Why? He knew he should have watched her pack and escorted her to the highway. "You lay a finger on her you coward, and I'll hunt you down."

Mendenhall laughed. "Does that mean you'll be there?"

Andy hung up on him.

When the highway intersected a county road, the SUV turned north. After ten miles, Mendenhall turned southeast at a fork that took them back toward Elmwater over a bouncy, ungraded dirt road.

"This is our escape route?" Hanania complained.

"We can't go back through town," Mendenhall said. "Everyone outdoors will see the rocket take off. Besides, no one will see us leaving this way. So what if we have to go slow in a few places?"

At a dead and splintered tree, they headed straight east six miles to the site. They parked behind the limestone outcropping a good fifty yards from the silo. Sixty yards of two cables lay in the grass. The men opened the tailgate and pulled the cables closer to the SUV and the huge truck battery that sat inside.

"Light westerly winds all the way," said Amin. "She'll travel above the jet stream so the winds won't affect her much. The target is a thousand feet lower than our current elevation. Perfect for my detonation switch. I'll set the controls."

Washington's current barometric pressure was 30.07 inches of mercury. The city's elevation above sea level was 400 feet. The men used the crane to open the nose cone. Asim popped out the bubble switch and set the altimeter to detonate at 1,400 feet above the ground over the target. Three centimeters separated the contacts on the switch. With the current barometric reading inputted, the device would snap shut at the desired elevation due to the greater atmospheric pressure nearer sea level, and whatever was under the bomb would vaporize in an inferno.

Asim proceeded to set the settings for the directional vanes on the tail fins. Vertically launched, once the rocket was a mile aloft into its flight, the motors would activate the vanes to rotate the rocket on an 88-degree trajectory from magnetic north, essentially due east. The rocket would climb 120 miles above the surface of the earth before engine burn out at which time it would be moving at 2 miles per second and gaining speed as gravity and momentum carried it on the final leg of its flight.

Asim removed the wooden safety plug from between the bubble switch contacts. He removed the neutron deflector from between the two halves of uranium spheres. Then he closed the shell tamper and bolted it shut to enclose the bomb within the steel housing. The men closed the nose cone and bolted it to its base. They loosened the cables holding the overhead cranes in place, turned on the motors to the wheels on each side of the hole, and drove the cranes off the silo opening. Everything was ready to go.

"We'll know soon enough," Mendenhall replied. The radio should broadcast news about an explosion long before we get to Omaha.

"Just taking the Americans by surprise is exciting," Hanania said. "They may know something's coming at the last minute, but they won't be able to do anything about it."

They listened as a radio news feed announced the President had left the White House for the ride up Pennsylvania Avenue to the Capital Building. "Just a few more minutes," Mendenhall said. He was in control of his body. His muscles were taut. Nevertheless, he was nervous. If this were successful, the leaders in Libya would praise him, even worship his intellectual and organizational prowess. The attack on the World Trade Center would go down in history as nothing more than a blind stab that knocked over a few buildings. If this mission were successful, the deaths and property destruction would be multiplied by a hundred – even a thousand. But if it failed—if he failed, he would be hunted across the globe.

Dusk was settling as the three men saw a vehicle rolling toward them in the distance. Hanania drew the 9mm pistol from his waistband and held it behind his back. They recognized it as a four-wheeler, and its lights came on a quarter mile away from them. The time was 6:40 p.m.

"Wait," Mendenhall said. "It's the guy I called. I want him here."

Andy pulled within twenty yards of the SUV with Tipper curled up behind him on the rack. He had so hoped he would never have to return to this site. He had to return even without Romme's pleadings because now they had Missy.

"Evening, gentlemen," Andy gave his words a slow country drawl. "So this is the night for the big test. Andy could hear a radio, but couldn't make out the broadcast.

"What's Romme doing? Mendenhall asked.

"Sitting in jail. He's getting out tomorrow. He wants to talk to you."

Mendenhall didn't respond but kept checking his wristwatch.

Romme was right. They were going to wait until at least 7:00 before they launched. But that time was fast approaching. He would have to make his move soon. "Okay, I'm here. Where is she?" Andy could see a broad smile from Mendenhall in the lengthening shadows of dusk. He knew every word that came from Mendenhall's mouth would be a lie, but he had to get him talking.

"Come over here. She's right here in the truck. I'll let you see the controls to the rocket."

"Let her go. She has nothing to do with this, and she can't tell anyone anything because she doesn't know anything."

"I'll make that trade. You for her–just until we get out of here. Then I'll let you go. She can drive that scooter of yours back into town."

Andy stepped out from behind the wheel and kept the four-wheeler between him and the SUV. Hanania watched Andy's every move. Mendenhall and Asim huddled on the far side of their vehicle. At the same time, Andy pulled the 9mm from beside the seat and slipped it into his pocket, then walked to where he had a better view of the back of the SUV. Making a trade, him for Missy, was a bald-faced lie to get him closer. He dared not get too close to any of them, but he had to get close enough to the back of the SUV to keep the ignition circuit from being completed. Andy kept inching forward.

Rather than being quiet about the launch, when the time had come, Mendenhall and Asim became loud and excited.

"Praises, praises," Asim chanted.

"Death to infidels," Mendenhall cried as adrenaline-laced blood rushed through his body with the power of a swollen river. He picked up the two cable leads and lifted his head to the heavens.

Andy reached in his pocket. The gun felt sticky. He had to act. Now was his only chance. He couldn't shoot him. He couldn't kill a man in cold blood. He'd have to rush the truck, dump the battery, pull the cables away. Andy prayed the rocket would not launch, would sit dead in the silo, sabotaged by his hand. But he couldn't take that risk.

Mendenhall turned to the battery.

The words finally came. Andy yelled, "Stop!" His gun was out and pointed at Mendenhall. Hanania fired. The bullet hit Andy in the left forearm. Tipper rushed Hanania and was on him in a second.

Andy fired. Mendenhall winced and fell against the tailgate. He clamped the first cable clip on the electrode and pushed himself up with his right hand to connect the other. Andy fired again and heard the distinctive whop of a bullet striking metal. Asim ran for the driver's seat of the SUV. Mendenhall fell forward. A spark flew as the cable made contact, but the connection failed. Andy ran at the truck dangling his left arm. With two hands, Mendenhall squeezed the final clamp and snapped it on the electrode. Andy hit him like a linebacker colliding head-on with a ball carrier and knocked him ten feet across the ground. But too late.

A rumble came from within the silo. A hiss, a roar, the ground at the mouth of the silo brightened as though the sun were announcing a new day. The nose cone rose, and the cylinder roared out of the ground. When the exhaust cone cleared the hole, the landscape became brighter than the sun at noon. Everyone was barely outside the danger zone of the blast. The heat was scorching. Prairie grass caught fire. The missile rose and gained speed. Within seconds it was a mile in the air. Still quite visible, but getting smaller as it climbed into the sky.

Andy turned to his snarling dog. Hanania's gun was in the grass. Andy grabbed the gun. "Tipper, Come!" The dog let go, and Hanania dashed for the SUV. Then came the sound that kicked Andy in the chest harder than any bullet. "Andy, help me," came a woman's scream.

With the tailgate still open, Hanania jumped into the vehicle. Andy tried to run for it, but the SUV was moving. The battery bounced out the back. The overhead backdoor waved and grated on its hinges as the SUV bounded ahead.

Mendenhall groaned, rolled back and forth in the dirt. He'd taken the bullet in his side. Andy knelt beside him and rifled his pockets, rolled him over and frisked his back. "Where's the transmitter?" Andy shouted as he rolled the man over.

Mendenhall tried to laugh. "It's gone, long gone," Mendenhall choked. "Asim has it. He would have pushed it as soon as the rocket took off."

Mendenhall lay back in the dirt choking and laughing.

Andy's left hand throbbed. He glanced at his arm. His shirt sleeve was soaked. Blood dripped from his finger. But there was no time to attend to himself. He jumped on the four-wheeler and gunned it after the SUV with Tipper on all fours riding the rack. He wanted to call the police station to stop the SUV if it came through town, but he couldn't drive and phone at the same time. He could see the tail lights ahead. The two men and Missy were a long way ahead, but if he could stay on their tail. If they harmed her in any way, he would gut them like catfish and never be the least bit remorseful.

The SUV headed past the turn that would take them to the road into town. Andy saw the rear lights giggle as the truck took the ditch beside the dead tree and instead of turning toward town, turned north up the old back road. Andy had the four-wheeler at full throttle. Tipper's head extended over Andy's shoulder. The dog braced, taking every bump and turn without the slightest loss of balance. Within seconds, they were at the old back road, too.

The SUV had the power to make it down the rutted road, but not the nimble agility. Asim floored it to cover distance but slammed on the brakes when ruts appeared. The SUV stepped sluggishly over potholes. Instead of manic starts and stops, Asim would have made better time keeping the vehicle to fifteen miles an hour. But his driving only slowed them down, and Andy was on their tail.

The four-wheeler sped around holes and over ruts at maximum speed. Within minutes he was upon them. He fired two bullets at the left back tire Andy fired a third shot near the driver's door and hit the side mirror with a clank that tore it from its mount. The SUV jerked left, then right. Asim drove into the ditch. The chase was over. Andy jumped for the back door, but it was locked. By the time he ran around to the other side, Hanania was in the backseat. He had a knife to Missy's neck and pulled her from the SUV.

"Drop the gun, or I slit her throat from ear to ear," Hanania said.

Andy didn't look into Missy's terrified eyes. He kept his gaze on Hanania. He pulled his left arm tight to his chest and took a few seconds to catch his breath. Then in a voice rich and authoritative, Andy spoke in a way that no one who heard his words would question their absolute sincerity.

"You don't want to die. If you were willing to be a martyr, you wouldn't have made a run for it. Stay here, and you'll be captured and pay for whatever destruction that rocket does. Is that what you want?" Andy didn't wait for any answers. "The next town is only a few miles from here." Andy lied and pointed north. They had eight miles to go to get to the improved county road, and ten more miles from there to the next town."Go for it now, and you may get away. Hurt her, and you'll die where you stand."

"Let her go," Asim pleaded. "Our mission has succeeded. Let's make a run for it."

Already Asim was moving up the road.

"Give me my gun," Hanania said.

"No gun. Let her go."

"You'll shoot me."

"I have no reason to shoot you. Release her, and I'll let you go."

Hanania took the knife away from her throat, turned, and ran to catch up with Asim.

Missy ran into his arms.

"Come, we must go. I have to get to the jail." Without any further coaxing, Missy jumped on the back of the four-wheeler and clung to Andy's waist. Tipper broke into a full run as they sped toward town. Andy flew past his farm into town, slamming the vehicle to a stop in front of the police station. He busted into the front office. Officers Bradford and Zang were on duty and jumped when the door flew open.

"Get that sonofabitch out here," Andy pointed to the cell block.

They both saw his bloody arm. "Andy, what happened?"

"No time for that. This town is in danger. Get him out here."

"But, Andy."

"Now! We've got to make him talk."

Officer Bradford grabbed a first aid kit.

"Out here?" Zang could hardly speak.

"Yes! Cuff him and have your Taser ready."

"Wait," Bradford said. He tore open a thick bandage with gauze ties. "You've got to get something on that." A congealed mass of a black clot filled the bullet wound.

"What happened?" Zang asked again.

"I got shot. I'll live. Hurry up."

As Bradford dressed his wound, Zang went in the cell block and brought Romme out handcuffed to a chain about his waist. Zang pushed Romme into a chair against the wall.

"Okay, Mr. ex-Army," Andy said, "I'm going to ask you once and once only. What's that transmitter all about?"

Romme's face fell, but he remained silent. Two seconds later, Andy hit him in the jaw with a right hook that knocked him out of the chair. With two hands, Andy smacked the chair upright on the floor. He hoisted Romme up, slammed him back into the chair, and clamped his good hand on his throat. "Mendenhall's shot up at the site, but the damn thing blasted off. Two other men got away with the transmitter. It's been activated. So if you know anything to save your ass, you better tell me now."

Romme strained at the cuffs that held his hands. "I'll string you up by the ankles and use you for batting practice if you don't talk," Andy said. He pulled back his fist.

Romme flinched and ducked his head. "Don't hit me again," he pleaded. "In the new elevator–at the top. There's another atomic bomb." Missy and the two officers inhaled audibly.

"You stay here," he said to Missy. Andy was out the door. He gunned the four-wheeler toward the Co-Op. When he reached it, he heard the wailing of a squad car behind him. He grabbed a pair of wire cutters and ran to the building. Buckets five feet apart were on a vertical conveyor belt outside the elevator wall that took grain to the top and dumped it. Andy saw the switch on a pole and snapped it into the on position. Nothing happened. It was the wrong switch, or the electricity wasn't on. He didn't have time to look around. An enclosed ladder ran up the side of the building to an opening near the top. He drove the four-wheeler under the ladder and jumped to the lowest rung.

Fire burned in his left arm. He forced himself to pull up to where he could grab the next rung. He couldn't feel his fingers, but he forced them to work. He ignored the pain. He had one thought. He must climb to the top, find the apparatus, and disarm it.

The roof was unfinished. The concrete walls were curing, and an open sky of starlight was Andy's view at the top. A maze of steel girders composed the roof support. One set of beams came down from the walls about three feet below where the curve of the roof began. Those beams were welded at a central hub. Another set of beams went up from the outer walls connecting at a central hub at the top that defined the upper shape of the roof. Andy saw what appeared to be a box resting on the lower hub.

Again there was a space he had to overcome. He would have to jump from the ladder through the open roof to the lowest I-beam. He could grab the beam, but could he hold on? It was at least 100 feet to the concrete floor below. He had to try. He didn't look down. He didn't try to psych himself up. He stood on the top rung – and jumped. His fingers caught the edge of the I-beam. With his last ounce of strength, he embedded his fingerprints in the steel beam, swung his legs up, and leg locked the beam. With his good right arm, he pulled his body on top of the girder.

High in the grain elevator, the January evening felt colder, yet sweat dripped from his forehead. Rising exhaustion seeped into his entire body. But the brilliance of the stars that shone through the open roof gave him light and an infusion of determination. He shimmied down the I–beam to the central hub.

There he found a hard plastic case complete with a handle and snap closures. He opened the box, and he saw the bomb. He heard the ticking. He saw no clock or read out, only the ticking. Steady, constant, like the click of a metronome set to one click per second. There were two halves of metal, round in shape, the edges of the half-shells facing each other, surrounded by charges and wires. Fuses to the charges ran to a central box. But he saw nothing distinctively a battery. Andy knew if it went off, it would shred the reinforced concrete walls of the elevator like tissue paper, level the town, and kill every living thing for miles around.

The maze of wires was perplexing, confusing. What if he cut the wrong one? What if just by snipping a wire a spark of current flowed setting it off? The notion of creating a spark was terrifying. Even if the radioactive material didn't implode, he'd still be a dead man from the detonation of TNT.

"Have you found it?" came a call from the elevator floor.

"Yes, it's here and its ticking," Andy cried.

"They're turning on the conveyor belt. Help is coming."

"Get back! Get out of here." Andy leaned back

against the girder to catch his breath. He could think of only one possibility. The bomb had to implode precisely, all charges going off at the same instant. He didn't know how the atomic reaction took place, but he knew the detonation required precision. He pushed the open case up a girder until the space between beams was wide enough, and he pushed the bomb over the side, It crashed one hundred feet to the floor below. Andy fell back in the nest of the girders, panting, utterly exhausted. Less than a minute later, the elevator floor exploded. The uranium chain reaction had been rendered harmless, but the TNT charges had remained connected to the timer and ignition source. The explosion blew out a two-foot-high chunk of the elevator wall a third of the way around the silo. For a few seconds, smoke rose, and the elevator held firm. Then it began to tilt and gave way toward the damaged side. The elevator collapsed in a massive crash of concrete and steel beams. Chunks of concrete on the wall behind him hit Andy as he was thrown over a hundred feet into the field beside the Co-Op.

CHAPTER THIRTY-ONE

THE ROCKET MAINTAINED a continuous climb. The yellow spot of exhaust fire grew smaller and smaller. The flight path didn't bend; the rocket didn't roll to a set course. The westerly wind and the rotation of the earth would push the missile to the east, but to anyone who saw the launch, it appeared to fly straight to heaven.

The flight controls hadn't activated. The directional flight fins on the rocket didn't work. The projectile flew directly above Elmwater, straight into the sky. It had the thrust to climb 660,000 feet in an arc to Washington D.C., but in a straight, vertical climb, it wouldn't go as high.

Hundreds of people in Northeast Kansas saw the bright exhaust plume in the sky. Some thought it was a shooting star. 911 switchboards lit up in towns for miles around. Was it a meteor? Was it a UFO? City sirens began blaring from Topeka to St. Joseph to Kansas City. Thousands of binoculars and telescopes scanned the night sky.

Then something reappeared. The fireball had gone out but could be tracked as it blocked starlight along its path. With a flight time just under fourteen minutes, the rocket's burnt-out remains crashed to earth in Northwest Missouri in a field between Interstate Highway 29 and the Missouri River. The jet stream and the rotation of the earth had pushed it 100 miles east of the launch site. Only the fins were recognizable as being from an aerodynamic projectile. The charred carcass of the rocket left a blackened hole the size of a house. The site was radioactive, but the bomb was a dud. The missile didn't descend to a low enough elevation to trip the bubble switch ignition. Picking through the debris the next day, HAZMAT technicians in protective gear collected the broken pieces of radioactive material and placed them in lead-lined cases.

The origin of the launch was quickly determined. The Kansas Highway Patrol arrested two men attempting to escape the area on foot. Another man was found wounded and unconscious near the launch site. A fourth man, currently in custody, was identified as being one of the conspirators when Del and Warren pointed him out as working with the wounded man from the launch location.

Mendenhall spent three days in the hospital in and out of consciousness. When conscious, he babbled in a state of delirium, seldom lucid, always in pain. Andy's bullet had ripped through his guts and destroyed the lower portion of his liver. At the end of day three, he died. But not before he learned that his scheme, his entire effort had been a complete failure.

Romme, Asim, and Hanania would spend the rest of their lives behind bars. In a way, it was a blessing. Had they ever set foot outside a maximum security prison, they would have been dead in a matter of hours.

Numerous interrogations ensued. Everything led back to Al-Quaeda in Lybia. By the time the U.S. military finished a three month attack and destroy operation, there wasn't a safe rat hole for a terrorist to hide in that failed country.

IT WASN'T THAT LATE when the elevator fell, a few minutes past nine. Anyone who had gone to bed was awake from the constant scream of sirens. By the time the TNT exploded, and the elevator collapsed, half the town was down by the Co-Op being held back by the police and volunteer firemen. Everyone knew Andy was inside the elevator. The explosion dropped everyone to the ground, but they were up, sprinting into the debris even before the dust cleared. Andy was unconscious, covered in shards of broken concrete. A steel beam lay across his back. His head was bleeding, and his pants were torn. His right leg bent at a crooked angle. They carried him out on a stretcher and whisked him to the hospital.

Missy paced the floor in the waiting area, only steps from the emergency room. She heard the chatter of voices, the bustle of footsteps. The door to the emergency room rocked on its hinges as nurses came and went. Rita Crenshaw came in the back door and hugged her. They talked in hushed tones. Gerald and Mae Morgan came in right behind Rita. They sat across the aisle from the two young women. Each of them quiet, heads down, hands folded and absorbed in individual thoughts. Gerald put his arm around Mae.

Dan and Jake came in and stood along the wall. Farmers more than five miles away heard the explosion. When they learned what had happened, they came into town with their wives: Grady, Bates, Michaels, and Galen Cecil, Nate Davis, Matt White, and more. Ethel Akers came in and hugged Missy, then sat with Evelyn Keaton and the Collins and the Beckers. Police officers Bradford and Zang stood inside the door. Chief Stevens would have been there, but he had to stay at the elevator where components of the bomb were being photographed, collected, and sealed for transport to Kansas City. The clock struck midnight, and everyone waited – quietly – patiently. No one left, but more people arrived.

Bill Grayson and Sheila Reynolds walked into the waiting room hand in hand and stood by the door of the hospital's small chapel. Del arrived with his wife, who used a walker, and one of the men offered her their chair. The stairs to the upper level of the hospital were filled with townspeople patiently waiting for news on Andy's condition. Half the town was in the waiting room or milling about outside.

At a quarter past 1:00 a.m., a doctor came out. He first looked at Gerald, who nodded toward

Missy. The doctor approached her, and in a whisper asked her to accompany him.

Missy saw his eyes were wet. "You're his…?"

"Girlfriend, soon to be fiance," she said.

The doctor nodded. "We've done all we can do for him now. You can go in and see him. Stay as long as you want."

Missy walked into room #8. A dim bulb threw light up the wall at the head of his bed. Additional light in the room came from the numerous monitors hooked up to him. Bandages wrapped his head and left arm. His right leg was in a cast, ankle to the upper thigh, elevated by a chain. Missy stood by the bed and took his right hand in both of hers, then leaned down and kissed his cheek. "I'm here, baby."

He squeezed her hands. "I'm glad you're here," he mouthed without sound. Then he made a feeble effort to cough, and saliva dripped off his chin.

She leaned near his ear. "I'm so proud of you, baby. Everyone is proud of you."

"They doped me all up, but I knew you'd come," he said. The words came slowly but clearly. "I can't feel my legs. I can't feel much of nothing."

"You took a bad fall, baby. But you'll get better. I know. You'll be good as new. I'll help you all the way."

Andy pushed his head into the pillow so he could look directly at her. "I wanted to see your beautiful face." He tried to smile.

She couldn't talk but lowered her head and kissed his lips as warm tears fell on his face. He was her man. In the subdued light of the room, he appeared so sick, so weak, so broken. Tenderly, she kissed his cheeks, his eyelids, and his forehead.

"You know," Andy said barely audible and with great effort, "I always wanted some kids to run around that farm to feed chickens, and have pet goats – like that Carson boy. Every farm needs kids, don't you think?"

"Yes, every farm," she was sobbing quietly and turned her face away. Andy had been waiting for her, and now he was slipping away. Missy could tell – by the strength of his voice and the rate of his breathing. She was not alarmed. She had seen them pull him from the twisted elevator debris. He had been through so much. And yet, he summoned the strength to wait for her, to see her one more time, and say goodbye.

"I couldn't let another little boy die," his voice trailed off.

Missy could do nothing but hold him. The doctor had told her nothing, but now she understood the inevitable. The man she loved was only human. He had given his body without a moments' hesitation in sacrifice for others. The townspeople of Elmwater, his friends and neighbors already understood his sacrifice. That's why so many of them were at the hospital now at such an early morning hour. Missy would always admire him for his courage and selflessness, but she loved him because he was her Andy. She leaned across the bed, cheek to cheek, and held his hand.

"Do you love me?" he asked.

"Yes, baby. With all my heart. I've loved you ever since the day you sat with me in the park."

Soon, he was asleep, the rise and fall of his chest barely visible, the sound of his breath inaudible. When the heart monitor began to hum a steady tone, Missy kissed him one last time as a nurse rushed into the room.

Missy wiped her eyes as she walked out. To Rita, Gerald, and Mae, she said, "Call Mr. Edwards and tell him to take good care of him. I'll be in tomorrow to make arrangements."

"I'll drive you home," Gerald volunteered.

"No, that's all right," Missy said. "I'm not tired. "I think I might drive out to the farm. I want to be by myself for a while." And as she turned, everyone in the waiting room stood, the men removed their hats, and everyone made a path for her as she walked to the door.

ABOUT THE AUTHOR

Clifford Morris was born and raised in Southwest Kansas. He served with the U.S. Army in Vietnam. During a forty-year career as a salesman, at one time or another, he promoted almost everything under the sun. A long-time sports official and private pilot, he now spends his time playing the piano and writing fiction. He currently lives in Oklahoma.